"Is something wrong?" Dahlia asked.

Dahlia stood beside Grant, her face lifted as she searched his gaze.

Those eyes of hers saw too much. He couldn't bear for her to glimpse that lost part of him that had never quite recovered. He shook his head. All he wanted was to be a good father to his twin stepdaughters. But was he?

Though Dahlia smiled, her beautiful hazel eyes didn't have their usual twinkle. They locked onto his, freezing him in place.

"Would you like to go for a coffee?" Dahlia asked after a moment. She had more to say about him and the girls, he knew.

Grant was surprised by how much he wanted to say yes. "I should get the twins to bed," he said.

"May I help?" The sparkle flashed back into her eyes.

"You want to help with bath time? You'll get soaked," he warned.

"It's happened before. I didn't melt," Dahlia teased. "As long as you don't mind sharing them for a while."

Mind? He was delighted. "Don't say I didn't warn you."

Lois Richer loves traveling, swimming and quilting, but mostly she loves writing stories that show God's boundless love for His precious children. As she says, "His love never changes or gives up. It's always waiting for me. My stories feature imperfect characters learning that love doesn't mean attaining perfection. Love is about keeping on keeping on." You can contact Lois via email, loisricher@gmail.com, or on Facebook (loisricherauthor).

North Country Dad

Lois Richer

LOVE INSPIRED
INSPIRATIONAL ROMANCE

Recycling programs
for this product may
not exist in your area.

INSPIRATIONAL ROMANCE

ISBN-13: 978-1-335-44832-3

North Country Dad

First published in 2014. This edition published in 2022.

Copyright © 2014 by Lois M. Richer

For questions and comments about the quality of this book, please contact us
at CustomerService@Harlequin.com.

Love Inspired
22 Adelaide St. West, 41st Floor
Toronto, Ontario M5H 4E3, Canada
www.LoveInspired.com

Printed in U.S.A.

But if we must keep trusting God
for something that hasn't happened yet,
it teaches us to wait patiently and confidently.
—*Romans* 8:25

To the wonderful folks in Churchill, Manitoba,
who make the north country so much fun.

Chapter One

"We're orphans, just like Cinderella."

Dahlia Wheatley had forgotten how cute kids were.

"Not quite," she said with a smile. "You've got a daddy."

"Oh, yeah." The auburn-haired twins glanced at the man sprawled out in the seat across the aisle, chin tucked into his chest, stubbled jaw barely visible. They smiled and went back to coloring.

They'd scooted across the aisle forty minutes ago for a visit. Dahlia had encouraged them to stay and color with her markers while their dad slept. He looked weary, like a father who'd used every last ounce of energy to entertain his two young daughters.

Dahlia could almost pretend she was part of their family. For a moment, she let herself imagine smoothing that unkempt hank of dark hair off his forehead, then she caught herself.

She didn't even know the man!

"I'm hungry." The wiggly twin, Glory, looked at Dahlia expectantly.

"Me, too." Grace handed Dahlia her marker. "When do we get to Churchill?"

"Not until tomorrow morning. It's a long train trip."

"Because Canada's so big." Glory nodded sagely. "I'll get something to eat out of Daddy's bag."

"Let's leave Daddy alone." Dahlia lowered her voice, not quite certain why it seemed so important to her that they not wake him up. "He looks very tired."

"That's 'cause he's not used to us," Glory said. Dahlia thought the words sounded like something she'd overheard an adult saying. "He hasn't been our daddy for very long. Our real daddy died."

"So did our mommy." Grace looked at Glory with the most woeful expression Dahlia had ever seen. "She's in heaven, with God."

"I see." Touched by their grief, worried the two waifs would burst into tears, Dahlia thought fast. "I have a couple of chocolate pudding cups. Would they do?"

"Yes, please." Glory released the paper she'd

been coloring and climbed up to sit next to Dahlia. Grace flopped beside her half a second later.

Dahlia dug out the pudding cups she'd thrown in her bag before leaving Thompson to go back home to Churchill. Paying the high price for a plane ticket or enduring a lengthy train journey through Manitoba's north country were the only choices available to reach Churchill. It took stamina for adults to endure the seventeen-hour train ride. Undertaking the trip with two energetic kids was a gutsy move.

While the twins ate their pudding, Dahlia fell into a daydream about their sleeping father and the circumstances that had led to him becoming a father to the twins. A wet splat again her cheek snapped her back to reality.

"I'm sorry," Grace said, her blue eyes huge. "I was trying to scrape the bottom and the spoon snapped."

"You got it on her shirt." Glory reached out to dab the mess with a tissue. She ended up creating a huge smear.

"Thanks, sweetie, but I'll do it." Dahlia cleaned her shirt as best she could, knowing that the dark chocolate stain probably wouldn't come out of her favorite top. "All finished?" she asked, eager to get the plastic spoons and containers into the garbage.

"Yep." Grace licked her spoon, depositing a drop of pudding at the side of her rosebud mouth before she held out her cup. "Thank you." Her sister copied her.

"You're welcome." Dahlia stored the trash, then pulled out a pack of wipes. "Let's get cleaned up before your dad wakes up and wonders what happened to his cute girls."

As she wiped their grinning faces and tiny hands, the twins told her that they were moving to Churchill from a small town on the prairies where their stepfather had been a teacher. Dahlia wanted to know more about the handsome daddy, but the twins had other ideas.

"Can we call you Dally?" Glory asked. "It's a nickname. I like nicknames."

"My grandmother used to call me that," Dahlia told her. Memories swelled but she pushed them away. This wasn't the time.

"Will you tell us a story?" Grace asked as she snuggled against her sister. "Our mom used to tell us lots of stories. Sometimes Daddy reads them from a book." She tilted her head, her blue eyes intense. "Do you know any stories, Dally?"

"I might be able to come up with one." Dahlia spread the small hand-quilted cover the twins had brought with them from their seats. When they were covered, she waited for them to settle.

This was what she used to dream about—

kids, special sharing moments, someone on whom to shower the love she ached to give. Part of that dream had been a husband, of course. A man who'd love her as her ex-fiancé never had. A man perfectly comfortable with two little girls who couldn't sit still, for example.

At that moment, the man across the aisle opened his eyes—gray eyes that cool shade of hammered metal—and stared directly at her. A smile creased his full lips.

"Go ahead with your story," he said in a low, rumbly tone. "Don't mind me."

Dahlia swallowed. Most definitely a hunk.

"She's going to tell us a special story." Glory nudged her sharp little elbow into Dahlia's side. "Aren't you, Dally?"

"Sure." Dahlia swallowed to moisten her dry mouth and told herself to stop staring at the man across the aisle. *He wasn't smiling at you, silly. He was probably smiling because of a dream. You're dreaming, too.*

"Are you sleeping?" Grace reached up and turned Dahlia's head so she could examine it.

"No, honey, just thinking," Dahlia said, embarrassed to be caught in the act of admiring their father.

"Do you know Sleeping Beauty? We love Sleeping Beauty, don't we, Grace?" Glory bounced on the seat. "Tell us that story, Dally."

"Yeah," the man across the aisle said in that husky voice. "Tell us that one."

But Dahlia was hooked on his deep voice and beautiful gray eyes. She couldn't concentrate.

Then he cleared his throat and her good sense returned. Now was not the time for distractions. She had too much going on in her life. This was not the time to get sidetracked by nice eyes.

She forced her attention away from him and began her favorite fairy tale.

"Once upon a time—"

I need a wife. Someone like that woman.

Grant Adams glanced at the twins now asleep on either side of him, surprised he hadn't woken up when they'd moved back beside him. The woman across the way was an amazing storyteller, her voice soft, melodic, like a lullaby. He'd let it lure him back into his dream world where life wasn't so overwhelming.

But though it was late and the rest of the car was dozing, Grant wasn't sleepy now. He was nervous. They'd be in Churchill by morning and then his new life would begin. He couldn't shake the feeling that he was failing the twins by bringing them to such a distant place.

A wife would have brought enough activities to keep the twins from being bored during the train ride. She certainly wouldn't have let them bother other passengers, like the woman across the way. A wife would have known he'd need three times the snacks he'd packed.

A wife could show these children she loved them.

Not that Grant didn't care for the twins. He did. Dearly. But he didn't know how to be a father. He didn't have the fatherhood gene—that's why he'd avoided love and marriage. That's why he'd vowed never to have children. Because he didn't have what it took to be a dad.

He'd studied enough psychology to know his lack of skill had to do with his mom walking out on his seventh birthday and leaving Grant with an embittered, angry man who drank until he was abusive. Grant had quickly learned to keep out of his dad's way, to not cause a fuss. None of this had earned him that special bond other kids had with their fathers. After a while, he had given up trying to find it and left home with an empty spot inside that craved love. Two failed relationships later, Grant knew he couldn't love. He'd vowed never to marry, never to have kids and expose them to the loveless childhood he'd endured.

Until Eva.

Eva of the sunny laughter and ever-present smile. Eva of the strong, unquenchable faith in God. Eva the optimist. After an entire year of persuasion, he'd finally accepted her love and her assurance that she could teach him how to be a husband and father. How could Grant *not* have married her? How could he *not* have adopted her two adorable girls?

Pain pierced his battered heart. He'd been naive to believe God would let him have so much blessing in his life.

Eva's death from a brain aneurism just six months after their marriage had decimated Grant. He'd never imagined that God, the loving God Eva had talked about, would take the one person who'd finally loved him. Losing his job a few months later had stolen every scrap of faith Grant had left.

So how could God possibly expect *Grant* of all people to be a father?

"You look like you could use a cup of coffee."

Grant lifted his head and saw the woman from across the aisle who had told the twins a story full of princesses and happily-ever-after. This particular princess had long red-gold hair that tumbled in a riot of curls around her face and down her shoulders. He realized suddenly that it was the exact same shade as the twins'. She had pale features like those the Italian Renaissance masters had smoothed from rare alabaster. But it was her smile that captivated Grant—wide, generous and inviting, it chased away the chill on his spirit.

"Maybe you don't like coffee," she said when he didn't respond. Her smile faltered, a tiny frown line forming between her hazel eyes. "I'm sorry if I bothered you."

"You didn't." Grant smiled and eased one hand free. "I'd love a cup of coffee. Thank you."

"I hope you're not just saying that to make me feel better." Her smile returned when he shook his head. She handed him the cup with a twinkle in her eyes. "You've sure got your hands full. Your twins are adorable."

Grant took a sip of the coffee. Earlier, he'd noticed a dark stain on the woman's emerald-green shirt, and a smudge on Glory's cheek to match it. But she wore a blue top now. Grant felt a stab of guilt at the thought that she must have changed clothes. She looked refreshed and awake. Beside her, he felt sticky, tired and utterly weary. And he had hours to go until they finally arrived in Churchill.

"How old are they?" she asked.

"Five."

"Glory and Grace." She sank into her seat across the aisle. "Wonderful names."

"I didn't choose them," Grant admitted. "I'm just their stepfather. Grant Adams."

"Hi, Grant. I'm Dahlia Wheatley. I own the hardware store in Churchill."

"It's nice to meet you." He squeezed the words out, trying to hide his shock. *Hardware?* He could not think of a vocation less likely for this delicate-looking woman. Ballerina seemed more appropriate.

"I'll confess, I guessed why you're on the way to Churchill. Laurel Quinn is a friend of mine." Dahlia smiled at him. "She mentioned she'd soon have a new employee at her rehabilitation project. She's eager to have you start work. The boys seemed excited about you when she told them. But then I guess most pre-teens are excitable." She grinned.

"Lives Under Construction is a great name for a project for troubled boys." Grant wondered how involved Dahlia would be with his workplace. "I'll only be working there on a part-time basis, but I'm looking forward to getting started."

"It's a great project. Once the boys figure out that the court did them a favor by giving them a chance to straighten out their lives instead of being locked up in a jail, they usually come around. Laurel will be glad you're early," she added. "Her newest group has already arrived. You'll be able to meet with them before they start school."

"I wanted to get to Churchill before September because the twins will be starting school, too."

"They're both clever. They'll do well." Dahlia's face softened as she glanced at Grace and Glory. "Laurel's rehabilitation program for troubled boys—we call it Lives—has gained a lot of recognition in the Canadian legal system." Her voice proclaimed her pride. "There never seems to be a shortage of kids needing help. Fortunately that's what they get at Lives, and now you'll be part of it."

"I was surprised Lives is so far into Canadian north, but I suppose isolation is one of the reasons for the program's success," he mused.

"I guess it helps that the boys can't easily escape," she teased. "But Lives' success is mostly due to Laurel." Dahlia's hazel eyes glinted with gold as she studied him. "The building used to be an old army barracks. Her biggest asset though is the land. She can expand as Lives grows."

"So she has plans for the place?" he asked.

"A lot. Laurel mentioned you're a life skills coach?" When Grant nodded, Dahlia admitted, "I'm not sure I know what that means."

"It means I'll be coaching the boys to figure out what they want from their futures," he explained, "and hopefully help them discover how to get it without breaking the law again."

"I see." Dahlia nodded, but those hazel eyes telegraphed her reservation. "Is that what you did before you came to Churchill? The twins said you were a teacher."

"Teaching life skills was part of my job as a high school teacher and counselor in a little town on the prairies." Grant tried to keep his voice light, refusing to show how frustrated he was with God's timing. "When they closed the school, my job ended."

"I'm sorry. I've heard that's happening a lot lately in rural areas." Sympathy shone in those amazing eyes. "No family?"

"I'm afraid my stepdaughters are stuck with only me." Grant glanced down.

"I'm sure they're lucky to have you." A soft look washed over Dahlia's face when her glance again drifted to the sleeping children. Then her mouth tightened. "Though if family doesn't offer the support it should, sometimes it's better to be alone."

Though Grant totally agreed with her, Dahlia's voice held a note of longing that made him wonder how her family had let her down. In fact, he'd begun to wonder a lot of things about this beautiful woman.

"How did you happen to end up in the hardware business?" A shadow fell across her face. "If that's not prying," he added.

"It's not. Anyone in Churchill could tell you and probably will if you wait long enough. Everyone knows everyone's business." She looked completely comfortable with that, but Grant's worry hackles went up.

What if everyone noticed his shortcomings as a father? Maybe then they'd think he couldn't work with the boys at Lives.

He desperately needed that job.

"Actually I'm—I *was* an architect." She paused and he knew there was something she wasn't saying. "I came to Churchill to be closer to nature while I do something worthwhile with my life." Dahlia made a face. "Does that sound all noble and self-sacrificing? It isn't meant to be. The truth is I left home after a split with my fiancé and my family. A friend told me about Churchill, and here I am."

Something about the way she said the words gave Grant the impression that there was a lot more to her story. He wanted to hear the rest, but he could hardly ask her to confide in him. They'd only just met.

"Judging by what I saw when I came for an interview last month, Churchill is an interesting place." Grant struggled to sound positive as a thousand doubts about this move plagued him again.

"Churchill is isolated, which makes it an expensive place to live," Dahlia conceded. "The winters are cold and long, and there aren't a lot of the conveniences people farther south take for granted. But there are tremendous benefits to living here."

"I'm sure," he murmured, while wondering what they were.

"We live with polar bears, belugas and a lot of other wildlife in gorgeous terrain," Dahlia bragged with a toss of her curls. "In case it doesn't show, I love Churchill. There's no place else I'd rather call home. If you give it a chance, I think you'll like it, too."

Since Grant and the twins didn't have anywhere else to go, he'd *have* to like the place.

"When we first left Thompson, I noticed you working on something." He hadn't wanted to ask before but now he glanced at the roll into which she'd stuffed her papers. "Blueprints?"

"Yes. Every year I sponsor a community project. This year I'm going hands-on with one at Lives." Her smile dazzled him. "Would you like to see my plans?"

She sounded so enthusiastic his curiosity grew.

Dahlia popped off the lid without waiting

for an answer. Her hands almost caressed the vellum as she unrolled it. She shifted so Grant could look without moving and perhaps wakening the twins. He gave the drawings a cursory glance. Surprised he took a second look then blinked at Dahlia.

"A racetrack?"

"Close." Her hair shimmered under the dim lights. She grinned with excitement as she leaned near. "It's a go-kart track," she whispered, obviously not wanting the other passengers to hear.

"Go-karts?" Grant frowned. "For the town?"

She shook her head slowly. "For the boys at Lives Under Construction. And their guests," she amended.

"Good for you." He wasn't sure what else to say. From what he'd seen of the place a month ago, Lives Under Construction needed some work. But somehow he'd never thought go-karts would be a priority. "Very nice."

"Don't ever try to fake it, Grant. You are so not good at it." Laughter bubbled out of her. She clapped a hand over her mouth to smother it, her eyes wide as she scanned the car to see if she'd woken any sleeping passengers. When she spoke again, her soft voice brimmed with suppressed mirth. "I know what you think. Go-karts are frivolous and silly, and they are. But they're going to be so much fun!"

Grant didn't know how to respond and Dahlia noticed. Her face grew serious.

"You don't approve." She sighed. "The boys are sent to Lives by the justice system to do time for their crime. And they should." She chose her words with care. "But many of them come from places where they've never been allowed to dream or imagine anything other than the life from which they've escaped." She gauged his reaction with those hazel eyes. "Do you know what I mean?"

"Fathers were in jail, mothers were in jail, kids follow the pattern." He nodded somberly.

"That, or they were beaten or abused, or forced onto the streets. Or any other horror you can name. Not that it excuses their crime." Dahlia's tone was firm. "But that's not my point."

Clearly Dahlia Wheatley had thought through her plan very carefully, but Grant couldn't figure her out. An architect running a hardware store who wanted to build a go-kart track for some problem kids.

Unusual didn't begin to describe this woman.

"I want to get the boys to dream, to visualize a future that they can create themselves." A wistful smile spread across her face. "I want these boys to reach for something more than what they've had."

"Why go-karts? I mean, how will go-karts help them do that?"

"I told you. It's a community project."

"But it's not really for the community, is it?" he pointed out quietly.

"In a way it's for the community." Her eyes darkened to forest-green, her frustration obvious. "I want to do it because there was a time someone helped me see beyond my present circumstances. And besides, this project will give the boys focus and keep them out of trouble."

"Has there been trouble?" In all his research about Laurel Quinn and Lives Under Construction, Grant had read nothing negative.

"Not so far," Dahlia admitted. "But the current group of boys is more troubled than previous residents at Lives have been. Especially one boy, Arlen."

As she nibbled off the last vestige of her pale pink lipstick, a thoughtful looked transformed her face.

"Arlen?" he asked.

"Yes." She slid the drawings back into the tube, then leaned forward. "Most of the kids in town have access to quads in summer and snow mobiles in winter."

"Quads? Oh, like all-terrain vehicles."

"Right. But the Lives boys aren't allowed to drive. Even if they could, Laurel can't have them taking off all over the countryside. She has to know where they are at all times. They are serving a sentence, after all."

"Right." Grant blinked at the intensity of her tone. She certainly was passionate about this project.

"A go-kart track would allow them some freedom as well as some fun," Dahlia added. "Lives sits on an old army base with a runway that I can clean up so it can be used as the track," she explained. "I've acquired some karts, too, but they'll need repair. The boys will have to figure out that part because I'm not very mechanical."

"I see." It wasn't a bad idea.

"When it's complete," Dahlia explained, a faraway look filling her eyes, "the boys could have a special day when they allow their town friends to use the track."

"Which would give them some esteem among their peers." At last he understood. "Clever. I like it."

"Then you'll help?" Dahlia said.

"Sure. If I can," Grant agreed, pleased to be part of something that didn't require making beds and trying to turn masses of red-gold auburn hair into what Eva had called French braids.

"Great! Thank you, Grant."

"I'm going to be busy." He glanced at the curly heads on either side of him. "There are these two, of course, and Lives. I'll also be working part-time as the school's guidance counselor."

"I'll be grateful for whatever time you can spare." Dahlia settled into her seat with a smile and sipped her coffee.

Grant let his gaze trail down her left arm to her hand. No ring. So Dahlia Wheatley was single.

If there were single women in Churchill, maybe he could find a wife. People still got married for convenience, didn't they?

Ordinarily Grant would have run a mile from the idea of remarrying. Eva had been his one and only shot at love and he'd lost her. But he wasn't looking for romance. He sure wouldn't marry to have children—he'd never bring a child into the world. But he needed a wife because he had no clue how to be a father. When it came to raising the twins, he was as hopeless as his old man. But the right wife would know how to fill in for his lack.

As Grant mulled over the idea of marriage, his eyes were busy admiring the lovely Dahlia. He wondered if she'd consider such a proposition. He had a hunch she was good with kids.

After all, he'd slept for over three hours and yet somehow there'd been no catastrophe or complaints. Dahlia's doing, he was sure. The drawings tucked into the seat backs and the smudge of marker on Dahlia's hand were signs that she'd known exactly how to handle them.

"Grant?"

He blinked and refocused on Dahlia, glad she could have no idea of his thoughts—otherwise she'd probably flee the train.

"I was thinking that maybe I could babysit Grace and Glory once in a while, in exchange for your help with my project." Her gaze lingered on the girls before it lifted to meet his.

"That would be nice." It surprised Grant just how nice it sounded.

"Good." She smothered a yawn. "Sorry. I'm tired. I think I'd better get some sleep before we arrive." After smiling at him again, she turned sideways in her seat, pulled a blanket over her shoulders and closed her eyes.

Grant wasn't in the least bit sleepy. Maybe coming here hadn't been a mistake after all. Maybe God was finally answering his prayer.

Glory murmured something and shifted restlessly. He stayed as still as he could, even though pins and needles were now numbing his arm.

Don't let them wake up yet, he prayed silently.

I'll never get them back to sleep and they need sleep. Please?

God answered his prayer as Grace automatically reached out and folded her hand over her twin's. Moments later, both little girls were still.

Grant glanced sideways at Dahlia Wheatley. He couldn't imagine anyone taking Eva's place. But neither was he capable of ensuring the girls had the home life their mother would have wanted for them.

Was Dahlia mother material?

He gave his head a shake. First things first. All he had to do right now was get to Churchill, and get their lives set up. He'd worry about Dahlia's part in their lives later.

Chapter Two

A face full of ice-cold water ended Dahlia's dream of a family of her own.

She jerked upright, lifting one hand to dash away the water droplets clinging to her chin. Grant's twins stood beside her with smiles on their chubby faces. "Girls, did you just throw water at me?"

"We saw that on television. Everybody laughed," Grace informed her. "The little boy behind you was crying so Glory said we should try to make him laugh."

Whoever was laughing, it certainly wasn't Dahlia.

"Please don't do that again. It isn't nice, okay?" She sat up and dried herself off as she best she could with her blanket.

"Where's your father?"

"He went to get us something to eat. We're

hungry." The two looked at each other mournfully.

"Did your father tell you to stay in your seats?" Dahlia asked.

"Yes." Grace looked ashamed.

"Then you should obey him."

When they'd taken their seats, Dahlia dug through her overnight case and found a clean, *dry* T-shirt. She'd have to change. Again.

"What's inside that round thing, Dally?" Glory asked, pointing to the tube with her plans for the go-kart track. "Treasure?" Her blue eyes began to glow with curiosity.

"They're special papers." Dahlia looked down the aisle for Grant's return. She waited as long as she could, but her damp silk top made her shiver. Finally she rose. "You two stay in your seats until your father comes back, all right?"

They nodded solemnly but Dahlia could see the bloom of interest flare across their faces and vividly recalled their earlier mischievousness. She'd just have to change her top in record time and get back before they got up to something else.

Easier said than done, especially after she caught sight of her reflection in the bathroom mirror. She released her damp hair from its clips and bundled it on the top of her head. Then she hurried back to her seat.

And stopped in the aisle, aghast. Nothing in her dreams of parenting Arlen had prepared her for this. Maybe she wasn't cut out to be a mother.

The air left her lungs in a gust of dismay. Her go-kart blueprints, her precious drawings, were spread on the floor. And the two little girls were coloring them.

Glory looked up at her and beamed.

"We colored it for you. Grace likes red, but I think roads should be black." She brandished Dahlia's black marker. "I mostly stayed in the lines."

What lines? The renderings were now obscured by every color of the rainbow, thanks to the markers Dahlia had allowed the girls to use earlier.

"I'm putting lines in the middle of the road," Grace said, the tip of her tongue sticking from the corner of her mouth as she drew long yellow stripes in what was once the middle of Dahlia's go-kart track. "Roads always have lines."

"What are these little things?" Glory dabbed at the icon for the go-karts with her marker, pressing so hard she went through the paper. Her bottom lip drooped as she saw the damage. "I broke it."

Grace carefully set her yellow marker on top of Dahlia's white jacket to embrace her sister.

"It's okay," she soothed, hugging Glory close. Then she looked up at Dahlia. "It's okay, isn't it?"

Dahlia took one look at those sad little faces and said, "Of course. It's fine, Glory. Now let's gather up my markers. We're going to be at Churchill soon."

She rolled up the blueprints and pushed them into the tube, pressing the lid on. Then she scooped the markers into their plastic case, ignoring the streak marring her white jacket. When the girls were once more settled in their seats, Dahlia scrounged through her bag and found two packs of crackers and cheese.

"I don't know where your dad is," she said, summoning a smile. "But why don't we have a picnic. A proper ladies' picnic," she emphasized when Grace began to climb down. "We have to sit nicely in our seats. Now we'll carefully open our snacks."

Of course the cheese and crackers didn't open properly and crumbs spilled everywhere. It seemed only seconds passed before the cheese and crackers disappeared—except for what covered their faces and hands.

"What's going on?" Grant stood in the aisle.

Dahlia noticed the lines of tiredness fanning out around his gray eyes. He was an exceptionally good-looking man despite his rumpled shirt and tousled brown hair. Not rail thin. Just nicely muscled with a dark shadow on his chin and cheeks. He wasn't as tall as some of her male friends in Churchill, which Dahlia liked. It always made her uncomfortable when someone loomed over her five-four frame.

"Um, what are you doing?"

Dahlia suddenly realized that they had the attention of all the other passengers. The morning was going from bad to worse. "They were hungry," she murmured.

"That's why I went to get them something to eat." He held up a bulging white bag, gray eyes cool as a northern snow sky.

"I figured that, but the twins were getting restless," she murmured. "I didn't think you'd want them disturbing others, so I let them have some cheese and crackers."

"Thank you. That was very kind, Dahlia. It's just that their mother didn't feed them processed food." Suddenly his gray eyes narrowed. "That's not what you were wearing before, is it?"

"No, I changed." She caught sight of Glory's face, her blue eyes were wide with worry. "Because I, uh, spilled some water."

"*You* did?" Grant asked, a hint of suspicion flashing in his eyes. "Did you spill water on your hair, too?" When she nodded, he glanced at the twins, then back at her. "I see. Well, thanks for helping them."

"No problem." She waited, shifting under his intense scrutiny.

He turned his focus on the girls. "I brought you fruit juice and a roll with jam."

"Mommy doesn't let us eat jam," Grace said.

"Well, you'll have to eat it today. It's all I could get."

Before Grant turned away Dahlia saw red spots appear on his cheekbones. The poor guy was trying, but the twins looked mutinous.

"I don't want it." A sad look fell across Grace's face. "I want my mommy," she wailed in a tearful tone as Glory joined in.

Those tears tore at Dahlia—she wanted to gather the girls in her arms and comfort them. But Grant simply patted Grace's head and clung to the bag with their breakfast while gazing helplessly at his weeping daughters. Glory, her face now streaming with tears, hugged her sister close and murmured reassurance.

Dahlia couldn't figure out Grant's reaction. He cleared his throat but no words emerged. He seemed confused. What was going on?

When it became clear to Dahlia that, for whatever reason, Grant wasn't going to comfort the girls, she stepped in.

"Hey, you two. Let's go clean up and then

you'll be ready to enjoy the breakfast your dad brought. Okay?" She lifted an eyebrow at Grant. For a moment Dahlia thought he'd refuse to let her escort them to the washroom. But before he could, the twins' sunny smiles returned and each grabbed her hand.

"Okay." They squeezed in front of her, heading down the aisle, chattering back and forth like young magpies. Dahlia held the door open, then glanced back at Grant. He was still standing where she'd left him, a bewildered look on his face.

Then he lifted his head and looked straight at her. She'd never seen anyone look so lost, so overwhelmed.

That's when Dahlia made up her mind.

She was a graduate of the betrayed-by-someone-you-trust-school and she had no intention of opening herself up to that again. But someone had to help Grant, and it might as well be her.

She'd step in—but only for the twins' sake.

When they returned from the bathroom, Grant was still standing in the aisle. Dahlia suggested Glory and Grace sit together, leaving Grant to sit in the empty seat next to Dahlia. The two girls dug ravenously into what seemed to Dahlia pitifully small and not very nourishing breakfasts, but then, she was no expert on feeding children.

"Is that what they usually eat?" she asked.

"They usually have a large bowl of hot cereal. Eva, their mother, always fed them nutritious food. I've tried to maintain that, but—" He sighed. "I can't always find it."

"Was your wife a vegetarian?" Dahlia hoped that didn't sound nosey. "My brother was a vegan. The doctor told my mom to make sure he got enough protein. Otherwise he was always starving."

Grant considered that for a moment. "I brought soup along for supper last night, but it didn't seem to satisfy them. I guess you noticed they were awake several times through the night." He sighed. "I'm new to all this."

"How long have you been at it?" she asked curiously.

"Eva died six months ago. We'd only been married nine months." He turned to glance at the girls. "She was so good with them."

"She had five years to practice," Dahlia reminded him. "You've only been a dad for a short while. Give yourself time."

"I'm not cut out to be a father. I've always known that." Grant's voice grew introspective. "But I didn't know I was going to lose Eva and have to parent on my own."

"I'm so sorry," Dahlia whispered thinking he

was lucky to have found love even though his voice betrayed the pain of his loss.

She thought he must have loved Eva deeply. She had seen the same kind of love between some of her friends in Churchill. But though she'd often longed for it, she'd never found that special kind of love for herself. Once she'd thought she had, but even then, even when she'd worn Charles's engagement ring, she'd never been certain he was the man God chose for her. And apparently she'd been right because Charles had quickly dumped her when she'd sold her shares in her family's architectural firm. He hadn't bothered to show up to say goodbye when she'd left Toronto either. No one had.

Eager to forget the past, she asked, "Was that why you came to Churchill, to get away from the memories?"

"I'll never get away from those." Grant glanced at the girls. "But at least in Churchill I'll have work."

It suddenly occurred to Dahlia that, because of his work as a counselor, Grant might be able to help with Arlen.

"Speaking of your work, can I ask you some questions about the boy I mentioned before—Arlen?"

"I'm not sure how much help I'll be since I don't even know him." Grant sounded guarded.

"Since you're a counselor, I thought you might have some insight. You see, Arlen's very troubled. Lives is his last chance," she explained. "If he doesn't get his act together in the next four months, he'll be moved into an adult facility."

"A penitentiary?" Grant frowned when she nodded. "What did he do?"

"Recently, he threatened some people, and vandalized their property. But before that he was a good kid." She looked at Grant closely. "I can't explain the connection I feel to this boy. I've prayed and prayed about him but—" She stopped, blushed. Grant was so easy to talk to. Perhaps—too easy?

"Go on," he encouraged.

"In your counseling—" Dahlia paused and summoned her courage. "Did you ever come across someone you thought was teetering on the edge, someone you were certain would tip one way or the other with the least provocation?"

"Yes." Grant's attention was totally focused on her now.

"You've run across someone like Arlen before?" she asked, relieved to hear he understood.

"The boy I'm thinking about became progressively more problematic for his teachers,"

Grant said. "He seemed almost driven to break the law."

At the sound of consternation from Glory, Grant excused himself and rose to mop up her spilled juice. Dahlia watched, unable to contain her excitement. Here at last was someone she could really talk to about Arlen. Laurel couldn't discuss a client, of course, and Dahlia's other friends didn't sense the desperation in Arlen that she did. But Grant had not only seen it before, he'd dealt with it.

"So what did you do?"

"Talked," Grant said. "A lot."

The air rushed out of her lungs, taking her excitement with it. "I've tried talking to Arlen. He doesn't hear me."

"I didn't mean *you* should talk." For the first time a genuine smile lifted Grant's lips, producing dimples in both cheeks that Dahlia found she couldn't ignore.

"What I should have said was that he talked and I listened," Grant corrected. "I encouraged, I tried to draw him out, I pressed him to expand on things he mentioned. Anything to keep a channel open between us." He shrugged. "In his case, talking eventually worked. He'd been brooding about things that he'd never resolved. Once he got them worked out, he saw he had options and that gave him courage to push toward the future."

"That's helpful." Dahlia nodded thoughtfully. "Thank you."

Grant studied her. In fact, his thoughtful gaze rested on her for so long, Dahlia felt herself begin to blush.

"Is something wrong?" she asked.

"I'm curious." Grant paused. "Is your go-kart project specifically tailored toward this Arlen kid?"

"It's a community project. I do one every year," she repeated. His eyes narrowed, but he remained silent. "Say what you're thinking." She knew she wouldn't like whatever was coming next.

"Maybe I made it sound easy to help that kid I told you about," Grant said. His serious gaze held hers. "It wasn't easy, Dahlia. It took months of work, for which I had trained. This Arlen—" He stopped, obviously uncertain as to whether he should voice his concerns.

"I am going to help him," she said with firm resolve. "I'm going to do whatever I can."

"That's good. He could probably use an adult on his side. But be careful." Grant laid his hand on her arm for emphasis. Immediately, a zing of reaction rippled through her and she caught her breath.

"You're not suggesting I back off?"

"No." He removed his hand. She edged away from his shoulder, hoping that would help her breathe more evenly. What was it about this guy that rattled her?

"I think you should be very careful. If he's smart, he's learned the system and mastered manipulation. He's probably figured out how to con his parents, probation officers, maybe even you. It might be too late for you to help him, Dahlia," he added in a soft tone.

"It can't be." She leaned back in her seat. She shouldn't have said anything. No one, not even her closest friends understood how desperately she needed to help Arlen. Why had she thought Grant Adams would?

A pair of giggles made her look across the aisle. Once, children like Glory and Grace had been what she'd longed for, what she'd prayed for every day. Someone to love. Someone who cared about her, whom she could care about. Someone to share with.

She'd had that connection with her brother. He'd always been the one she'd counted on to be there for her. But she hadn't been there for him. She'd let him down when he'd needed her most. He'd begged her to help him and she'd been too weak. Now he was gone. She missed him so much.

It was only since Arlen had come into her life that Dahlia had begun to hope again. She believed God would heal her hurting heart through caring for Arlen.

"Why is helping this boy so important to you?"

Those gray eyes of Grant's refused to let her avoid his question, but something in her knew that she could tell him the truth, that she could trust him.

"The reason it's so important to me to help Arlen," she began, "is because… I want to adopt him."

Grant wasn't sure he'd heard Dahlia correctly. "Adopt him? But I thought—that is, he's older than the usual age for adoption, isn't he?"

"He's thirteen," Dahlia said. "He's in trouble and needs someone who will be totally on his side."

A single woman adopting a troubled boy who was on the verge of becoming a teenager? There were so many ways in which this was a bad idea that Grant wasn't sure where to begin. He was about to voice his misgivings when he saw the sadness on her face.

Whatever Dahlia Wheatley's reason for helping this kid, he felt certain it stemmed from some emotional pain of her own, and he wanted to know what it was. He'd hardly known her an hour and yet already he wanted to make things better for her.

"Why does Arlen matter so much to you?" He hated the way her hazel eyes dimmed of joy. "Please tell me."

Dahlia glanced at the twins. Grant checked and noted they were playing one of the games they'd created together. He heard her inhale, gathering her courage.

"Because of my brother. Damon was my best friend. He was eighteen when he ran away from home."

"I'm sorry, Dahlia," he said, feeling the pain in those few words.

"He left because he couldn't live up to my parents' expectations." Her hazel eyes grew shiny with tears. "Even though Damon tried his best, he felt he could never be enough for them. They wanted an heir for their architectural firm, a prodigy. Damon wanted to paint."

"What happened?" Grant could tell there was more to the story just by looking at her.

"He was walking on the road at night. A car hit him. The driver left him there to die." As Dahlia exhaled, a sob escaped her lips. Then she dabbed at her eyes and sat up straight. She looked him in the eye. "It was my fault Damon left, my fault he died."

Grant resisted the urge to reach out and touch her, to comfort her. "How could it be your fault?" Grant knew this wound in her heart had festered for years.

"Damon died the night of my sixteenth birthday." A tear rolled down her cheek. "He'd had a big fight with my parents about his grades that afternoon. He asked me to talk to them, but I was too afraid to confront my parents." Her voice dropped with shame. "I was always too weak to stand up to them."

"Dahlia, there is no way a sixteen-year-old is responsible for her sibling. It wasn't your fault." But Grant knew he wasn't getting through to her. She simply gazed at him with that sad, weary smile.

"I was too weak to be there for Damon, but I *am* going to be there for Arlen." Her voice held fierce determination. "He's not going to be one of the lost ones. Not if I can help it."

Because they were getting close to Churchill, Grant decided to say nothing more. "I'm glad you told me, Dahlia," he said very quietly. "Your brother sounds like he was your best friend." She nodded. "Regarding Arlen, though, I need to think about the situation a bit before I give any advice. Okay?"

"I'd appreciate any advice you have to offer," she murmured. "Thanks for listening."

Grant nodded and moved back to his seat across the aisle while marveling at Dahlia's mother's heart. Then the girls cuddled against him, begging him to tell them again about their new home.

As Grant related what little he knew about the house Laurel had arranged for them, he was very aware of the woman across the aisle who was now gazing out the window as if she were a world away.

Grant wasn't sure exactly how, but he *was* going to talk to Dahlia again. He sensed she needed release from the pain of her past and he wanted to help her more than he'd wanted anything in a long time.

An architect. That fit. He could see her long delicate fingers drawing gorgeous houses or state of the art office towers. He could not see her weighing nails or discussing grades of oil.

Funny, but Grant could also see himself around her in the future, which disconcerted him. Still, there was definitely something special about Dahlia. Most women were bored to tears with him. They tried to get him to talk about himself, but Grant preferred to listen, mostly because it was safer.

But he had a sense that Dahlia was the kind of person who could get you to admit things before you even realized you had. He could see her as a wife, and as a mother. She was generous with the twins and made them laugh. That's what he wanted in a mother for Grace and Glory....

Grant shook himself out of his daydream. There were any number of reasons why he shouldn't be thinking of Dahlia in this way, not the least of which was she wanted to adopt this boy, Arlen. And if there was one thing Grant knew for sure about his new life in Churchill, it was that he wasn't going to subject any more kids to his parenting. Grace and Glory were all he could handle.

Chapter Three

"You must behave and not bother anyone," Grant told the girls as he got them ready to go to Lives Under Construction.

He felt foolish for having thought it would be easy to find a babysitter for the girls after only a few days in town. It was a mistake Eva never would have made. Now he resigned himself to the difficulty of keeping them occupied during his first session with the boys at Lives.

At least his car had arrived on yesterday's train so he could drive. Lives was situated just far enough out of town that walking there with two five-year-olds would be impossible.

"We'll behave," Glory promised.

"Put your crayons and coloring pads in your backpacks. You can work on those, but you can't interrupt. Okay?"

"Okay, Daddy." They nodded with serious faces.

Daddy. Why did he always feel like an imposter when they called him that? Maybe it had something to do with his most recent failures.

Today the twins had begun kindergarten. He'd been so busy setting up his office at the high school that he'd forgotten to buy their supplies. Eva would have made sure they were prepared, maybe even had their hair trimmed. Heaven knew Grant craved shorter hair for the twins. The endless combing, snarls, braids— all of it made him feel even more of a klutz. But he couldn't bring himself to cut those glorious curls.

Tomorrow he'd go to the northern general store and buy everything on the list the teacher had sent home for him. She'd been understanding, but Grant hated looking so incompetent. He doubted any of the other parents had sent their kids to school without supplies.

Then there were clothes. The twins were still wearing things they'd clearly grown out of. He should have stretched his funds, cut back more, done something in order to outfit them better, but he couldn't help that now. They'd have to make do until a paycheck came in, though everyone in town would probably be talking about the shredded knees of their pants. Add mending to the list of things he couldn't do.

When they got to Lives, the twins bounded out of the car, happy and excited. They'd taken to Laurel immediately when she'd appeared yesterday with a welcome cake, but Grant wasn't sure how Grace and Glory would react to the boys. Maybe he could get the girls to stay in the kitchen while he met with them.

"I thought we'd all sit around the kitchen table," Laurel told him, dashing his hopes as they walked in.

The boys were in the midst of enjoying a snack. Silence fell when he entered with the girls. As usual, Grace and Glory won over their audience quickly, and it wasn't long before the boys were plying the twins with food. When they were finished, Grant thought he saw regret on the boys' faces when he situated the twins at a table in the corner to color.

"Remember now, no interrupting," he reminded softly.

"We won't, Daddy," they chirped together.

"I'm sorry," he apologized to Laurel. "I don't have a babysitter yet."

"They're no problem. Now, let me introduce you properly," Laurel said. "This is David, Marten, Arlen, Kris and Kent. They're all new to Lives. This is Rod—he's been here for a while."

"Nice to meet you," Grant said, taking in details about each of the boys.

David, Martin and Kent were towheaded preteens who looked nervous and scared. Grant guessed they'd been talked into committing some offense and had been sentenced to Lives with the hope that one term would be enough to straighten them out. Kris stood next to Arlen, and had adopted Arlen's bored expression. It was an expression Grant had seen many times before. Rod was the only boy who looked perfectly comfortable.

"I'm Grant. I hope we'll all work well together," he said with a smile.

"What exactly are *we* working toward?" Arlen made no effort to conceal his surliness.

"Lives operates on respect, Arlen," Laurel reminded quietly but firmly.

"So you're the resident shrink," Arlen said, ignoring her.

"Life skills coach, actually," Grant corrected in a bland tone. "I'm here to help you figure out what you want in your future."

"Money, power, fame," Arlen joked. He grinned when Kris snickered but his eyes never left Grant.

"That's all you want?" Grant held the boy's glare. "It shouldn't take us long then."

"You think it's that easy to get those?" Arlen

barked a laugh then looked to the other boys. "Hey, this guy's got the secret to life."

"There's no secret, Arlen." Grant leaned back and studied the boy. "If you want money, you get a job. If you want fame, you do something notable. If you want power, you become a leader."

"Who gets rich from working a job?" Arlen sneered.

"Lots of people. They work, they save and they accumulate. Is money your goal, Arlen?"

"It's everybody's goal." Arlen stretched his legs out and leaned back in his chair.

"Actually, it isn't," a voice from behind Grant said.

Grant turned, surprised by the thrill he felt at the sight of Dahlia.

"Lots of people with money are very unhappy." Dahlia offered Grant an apologetic smile. "Sorry to interrupt."

The twins rushed to Dahlia, calling her name with glee. She hugged both of them, smoothed their hair and asked about the pictures they were creating.

"Hi, guys," she said to the boys. They all responded but one. "Hello, Arlen." She looked directly at the sullen boy. He ignored her. "I should have phoned first," Dahlia said, her gaze moving to Laurel. "I didn't realize you were having a session this evening."

"We're just talking." Laurel held up the coffeepot. "Want some?"

"No, thanks." Dahlia turned to Grant. "May I take the twins outside to play while you finish your discussion?"

"Sure." Grant noticed how ecstatic the twins were to be with Dahlia, how eagerly they followed her from the room. Was he giving them enough attention?

He waited for Dahlia to escort the girls outside before he steered the conversation back to money. The boys initiated a good discussion about the role of money in their lives, but Grant found he was distracted by the woman playing with the twins outside the big kitchen window.

After half an hour, Grant knew it was time to shut down the group session. He wasn't doing his best listening and the boys were tiring. He ended on a thinking point and after scribbling a couple of notes, Grant gathered his and the twins' belongings and said goodbye. When he stepped outside, squeals of laughter greeted him.

"You're it." Dahlia tapped him on the shoulder then raced away.

Grant stood in the twilight, a memory weighing him down. Games were not something his father had permitted. In fact, he'd downright disapproved of them. The one time Grant had tried to join a school football league, he'd been severely punished.

Keep your mind on your work, boy. You won't live here free forever.

Even now, the injustice of it burned inside. All through his childhood he'd slaved to keep the house clean and the yard tidy. He'd even learned to cook simple meals, which his father couldn't bother with once he'd gotten a bottle in his hand.

"Is something wrong?" Dahlia stood beside him, her face lifted as she searched his gaze.

Those eyes saw too much. He couldn't bear for her to glimpse that lost part of him that had never quite recovered from his father's brutality. He shook his head then touched her arm.

"You're it," he said.

Though Dahlia smiled, her hazel eyes didn't have their usual twinkle. They locked on to his and held as a fizzle of current zipped between them, freezing him in place.

"Would you like to go for a coffee?" she asked.

Grant was surprised by how much he wanted to say yes. But the twins danced at his side. "I should get them home to bed," he said.

"May I help?" The sparkle flashed back into her eyes.

"You want to help with bath time? You'll get soaked," he warned.

"It's happened before. I didn't melt." Dahlia teased. "As long as you don't mind sharing them for a while."

Mind? He was delighted. "Don't say I didn't warn you."

It turned out Dahlia had ridden her bicycle over to Lives, so Grant loaded it into his trunk. Then they headed home with the twins chattering all the way.

"I'm hungry," Glory announced to Dahlia. "We had beans for supper. They were yucky. Daddy forgot mommy's special spices."

"He burned my toast, too," Grace added with a baleful look. "Can I have not-burned toast before we go to bed?"

"We'll see," Grant said so that Dahlia wouldn't have to say anything. It was his favorite expression because he never actually had to promise anything. He didn't make promises anymore, not after promising Eva he'd raise her girls the way she wanted. Look how that was turning out.

"I'm not the world's greatest cook." Dahlia tossed Grant a smile. "But I can manage not-burned toast."

"Easy to say," he warned. "Just wait until you have helpers."

Dahlia laughed as if it was the best challenge he could have given her.

When they reached his house and she bounded out of the car, ready to face her test, Grant had two conflicting thoughts in his mind.

He liked this dynamic woman—a lot. And he'd be doing her a favor if he kept his distance.

Dahlia wasn't sure what she'd expected Grant's home to look like, but it wasn't this. An old sofa and a matching chair covered in a pretty chintz pattern framed a large coffee table, the perfect size for two little girls to sit at and color. In the corner a tidy desk nestled under the window. There was no dust and no mess, yet the room had a lived-in feel, as if people enjoyed each other here.

She allowed herself to be pulled through the house as the girls chattered about their first day at school. It was while Grace and Glory were showing her their room that Dahlia noticed how few clothes they had in their wardrobe. None of them looked warm enough for the cold northern winter that would soon arrive.

After a lively bath time, Dahlia made the girls cinnamon-sugar toast, which they devoured. Then she supervised toothbrushing, read them a story and tucked them into bed, conscious of Grant standing by, watching. As she was about to leave the room, she noticed that Grant seemed tense.

"Good night, girls," he said, his voice hesitant.

"Kisses first, Daddy," Glory reminded.

He dutifully bent so that each girl could embrace him, and waited patiently as they plastered kisses across his cheek. But when Grace tipped up her face for his return kiss, Dahlia's heart squeezed.

A look of pure panic spread across Grant's face. He hurriedly brushed his lips against Grace's cheek, and a second later, did the same with Glory. Then he quickly drew away.

A moment later, his composed mask was back in place. But Dahlia had seen the truth.

Grant Adams was scared of his daughters.

She couldn't think of a thing to say as they moved back into the living room. Grant made tea and poured it, carrying her cup to where she sat in the easy chair. After the silence stretched out too long, he tilted his head and studied her in a quizzical way.

"Why did you choose a hardware store?"

It was exactly the right thing to break the tension that had fallen between them. Dahlia burst out laughing.

"I'm serious. It's not at all what I'd have guessed you'd do," he said.

"It's not that far from architecture," she mused. "Once I drew plans to build things, now I sell goods to make plans come alive."

"But don't you miss the creative part of being an architect?"

"Not really," she said, only then realizing it was true. "I like the problem-solving aspect of running a hardware store." She looked directly at him. "Besides, I couldn't stay in the family firm anymore."

Dahlia knew he was waiting for an explanation, but she wasn't sure how much to tell him.

"You don't have to talk about it if it's painful," he assured her.

"It is quite painful." Dahlia cleared her throat, sipped her tea then began. "I trained as an architect because my parents expected me to join their architectural firm. They told me that since Damon was gone, I'd take over."

"You didn't want that?"

"I did, more than anything." She heard the fervency in her own voice and smiled sadly. "I had a lot of dreams for the company. My fiancé, Charles, and I used to talk about the things we'd change, how we'd grow the business." She looked down into her tea. "I had no idea my parents thought I was incompetent."

"But—" Grant raised an eyebrow.

"They wanted *Charles* as CEO. I would be a figurehead, to carry on the family name." The sting of it was as sharp as it had been four years ago. "I graduated top of my class, well ahead of Charles. I could have taken a fellowship with a prestigious Montréal firm. Instead I went home, because they 'needed' me."

Dahlia couldn't disguise the bitterness that shone through her words.

"Why would they do that?" Grant asked.

"Because I was too weak, or so they thought." Dahlia saw confusion on his face and decided to tell him the whole story. "I had cancer as a child. Despite the fact that I got better, my parents always considered me sickly. Fragile. The doctors said I was cured, but my parents never heard that. My entire childhood, they were always on the watch, protecting me from myself." She exhaled. "Thank goodness for my Granny Beverly."

Grant sat silently watching her, waiting. That's what made him good at his job, Dahlia decided. He didn't have to say a word because you could feel his interest in you.

"Granny Bev was a dragon. She suffered terribly from arthritis, but she came to see me every single day when I was in the hospital. And she always spoke the same message. 'You are strong, Dally. You can beat this. You can do whatever you put your mind to.'"

"Good ally to have," he murmured.

"The best." Dahlia swallowed the lump in her throat. "Because of her, I beat cancer *and* finished school on the honor roll, though I'd missed more than half the year. Because of Granny Bev, I ignored my parents' comments about being too delicate for gymnastics, too." She smiled. "I actually teach it now, twice a week. You should enroll the girls."

"Maybe I will," he said.

"I'm a pretty good teacher." Dahlia knew she sounded proud and she didn't care. It had been a long, hard road to silence those negative voices that had dragged her down, and she'd succeeded.

Almost.

"Tell me the rest of the story," Grant prodded.

"I fell in love with Charles at university. He said he loved me, gave me an engagement ring. I thought my life was on track." She made herself continue though she'd begun to wish she hadn't started this. Revealing personal details was not her usual style and defending herself even less so. "We both interned at my parents' firm. They loved Charles. They offered him a job when we finished school."

"Was he supportive of you?" Grant asked.

"At school, yes. And at first he was a great partner at work." She paused.

"And then?" Grant nudged.

"Then things began to change." The understanding in his eyes encouraged her to continue. "Meetings were changed without notifying me. My parents took me off three large commercial projects I'd brought in and gave them to Charles although his specialty had always been residential."

"You complained?"

"Vehemently. They said they were worried about my health. Charles didn't want me to be run-down for the wedding. To prove them all wrong, I went out and found three more major clients." She smiled wryly. "Didn't do me any good. I caught the flu, which turned into pneumonia. I was out of the office for a week. By the time I came back to work, Charles was acting CEO. I had been given the title of assistant."

Grant whistled. Dahlia nodded.

"My parents' explanation was that in two months they would turn the company public so they could retire and travel. They felt Charles was a natural for CEO, but he needed time to prove himself before a new board came in. I was to be the company spokesperson and find new clients, *because I was so good at it,*" she mocked. "I'd be a figurehead, but Charles was the boss."

"What did Charles do?"

"Charles pretended it was all a big surprise, that he hadn't put in a word here and there to make my parents doubt my ability. He'd always promised we'd run the company together, but from the first day I knew who was in charge and it wasn't me." She forced a smile. "He said to think of it as a merger that would be cemented when we married. Later I could stay at home and 'look after myself' while he ran things."

Grant tented his fingers under his chin but said nothing. Dahlia continued.

"It took just two weeks before my office was moved off the main floor and I lost all my clients. Charles said he was reorganizing, but I got organized right out. My parents wouldn't listen to me. In Charles they'd found the son they'd lost."

"So what did you do?" Grant asked.

"The day the company went public I bought as many shares as I could—enough to get me into the general meeting. The board suggested Charles as CEO. I publicly refused to support him and stated why. A vote was called. Granny Bev, who had also bought shares, voted with me. Charles lost."

"And your parents?"

"They were furious. I told them how disappointed I was that they'd treated me so poorly." She exhaled, brushed away a tear and continued. "I told them that I'd prove I am strong enough to build my life and that until they were ready to acknowledge me as a fully capable adult, I didn't want to see them again."

"And you haven't?" he asked when she paused.

"Granny Bev had a stroke the next day. I stayed with her until she died. As soon as her funeral was over, I left. I've never gone back." Dahlia had to stop for a moment. "Before she died, Granny Bev said to me, 'You are the strongest person I know. Live your life *your* way, Dally.' So that's what I'm doing."

He nodded, his eyes on her, watching, waiting.

"She left me her stock in my parents' company. I sold my stock to buy my store here. I've never regretted that," Dahlia added.

"And Charles?"

"I've regretted him many times, but I never heard from him again, which is just as well," she told him.

"So now you're determined to live by your grandmother's words," he mused. "You're proving you're smart and strong and capable."

"Yes." She frowned at him, hearing something underlying his words. "What's wrong with that?"

"Nothing at all. I'm just wondering if it's enough for you."

"What do you mean?" Dahlia found herself irritated by his words.

"I've seen you with the twins. I've listened to you talk about Arlen. You have a heart for kids. You love people. You *need* people." Grant paused, then quietly said, "Shutting out love because one man hurt you won't heal your heart."

"I have lots of love in my life," she replied defensively. "I have good friends. We support each other. And one day maybe I'll have a child, too. Perhaps Arlen."

"Will that prove your strength?" he asked quietly. "Will he be enough to heal the pain Charles and your parents caused?"

Dahlia stared at Grant. Images of the fairy-tale dream from her youth, one she'd never shared with anyone but Damon, played through her mind. A family, motherhood. A husband, laughter, love...

"I don't know what it will prove," Dahlia whispered. "I only know I can't give up everything I've worked for. I need to prove myself."

Grant didn't say anything for a long time. Tension stretched between them like a taut wire and finally, when Dahlia could stand it no more, she rose.

"I should go home. Thanks for sharing the twins' bath time with me. It was fun."

"Not a word I would have used to describe it, but you're welcome." He smiled as he escorted her to the door.

She started to say good-night, but instead, she asked, "After all I told you, aren't you going to say anything?"

"I'm not a judge, Dahlia. You have a right to live your life any way you want. I wonder though—" He paused, not taking his eyes off her.

"Yes?" Dahlia shifted under that stare.

"I wonder if you realize you just described love as making you vulnerable and weak."

Dahlia felt as if he'd somehow seen right into her heart. Without addressing his comment, she simply said good-night, took her bike from the driveway and rode away, aware that he stood there watching until she turned the corner. Her thoughts were on Grant and what he'd said.

She was embarrassed by how much she'd shared with him, but more than that, she was floored by his observation. Did she really see love as making her weak and vulnerable? She'd certainly been made to feel that way by her parents and Charles.

Then Dahlia wondered if Grant said that to her because he felt the same way.

She remembered the petrified look on his face when the girls were saying good-night to him and decided that whether he knew it or not, she wasn't the only one who needed help untangling feelings about love.

Perhaps they could actually help each other. Dahlia could offer him assistance with the twins, and he could help her get through to Arlen. Perhaps they could help each other get closer to love.

The question was, was it safe for her to spend time with a man who made her heart beat a little faster simply by studying her with those gray eyes that seemed to look right into her heart?

There was only one way to find out.

Chapter Four

"I guess I don't understand what Grant's doing," Dahlia admitted to Laurel. She glanced around Common Grounds, the local coffee hangout, relieved it was almost empty. She didn't want anyone to overhear. "He never says very much to them."

"Grant explained to me that he's trying to gain the boys' trust first, by listening," Laurel said. "It only seems like he's not doing anything."

"I didn't mean that." Dahlia shook her head. "I'm sure he knows exactly what he's doing with the boys. It's his daughters I'm referring to."

"The twins?" Her friend shook her head, her confusion evident. "Grant seems like a very conscientious father."

"He is. That isn't what I meant, either. It's just—" Dahlia sighed. Laurel was looking at her quizzically. "Don't you think he seems rather standoffish with the girls?"

"I haven't really seen him with them much but no, I've never thought that," Laurel said. Her forehead pleated in a frown. "Why? Do you think there's something wrong?"

"No, no." Dahlia wished she'd never said a word. "I've just noticed he doesn't show them much affection, though I suppose that could have something to do with his grieving process."

"Maybe he's not the affectionate type," her friend suggested. "It's obvious the twins love him dearly, so I doubt there's anything to worry about."

Dahlia didn't want to belabor the point, though her reservations remained. "I have to get back to work, but thanks for sharing coffee with me. I don't get out of the store in the afternoon very often."

"You should," Laurel encouraged. "You push yourself too hard."

"If I don't, who will?" Dahlia smiled, paid for their coffee, then hurried back to work. On the way she met Eddie Smart, one of the many miners who used Churchill as his home base.

"Hey, gorgeous. Are you free to have dinner with me tonight?" When she hesitated he added, "I'm going back up north to the mine in a couple of days."

"Oh, Eddie, I'm sorry. I'm tied up." Dahlia felt guilty for refusing again but she didn't want to add to the romantic thoughts she knew he harbored toward her. "Can I take a rain check?"

"Sure," he said good-naturedly. "I'll be back in time for the fall supper. How about we sit together at that?"

"I'll try," she told him, unwilling to commit. Eddie was sweet. She didn't want to hurt his feelings but she was not attracted to him.

As Dahlia walked toward her store, her thoughts returned as usual to her go-kart track. She decided to call Grant later to see if he could help her with it on Saturday. The weather was gorgeous but northern winters came hard and fast. She needed to get the project going.

As it turned out, Laurel took the twins leaf hunting for a school project early Saturday afternoon so Grant was free to accompany Dahlia on a survey of the road she wanted to use for the track.

"It looks in fair condition," he said as they walked the winding, paved road. "I wonder why it was made in a circle."

"I did some research on this old base." As they walked together in the warm sunshine, Dahlia basked in a sense of camaraderie. It was nice to have someone to help her with the go-kart project. Of course, Grant wasn't just *someone*.

"And you learned?" he prompted.

"There was a lot of suspicion in the fifties. Everyone feared invasion by the Russians so the airstrip here was maintained. When the base closed, they dismantled the long, straight runway so no enemy plane could land. I guess they figured this circular bit wouldn't be of use to anyone."

"It will make a good go-kart track," he said, studying the weeds and grasses that threatened to take over. "It's good that this area is fenced. No wandering polar bears. But it sure will need some cleanup."

"That's where the boys come in," she said with a grin. "They can put in some sweat equity. I'm hoping you'll help them see my vision." She winked at him then stopped, surprised by the freedom she felt with him.

"I'll try." Grant blinked then glanced away. He resumed walking, obviously preoccupied.

"Is something wrong, Grant?"

"I was just thinking that I need a better way to get through to the boys about what their futures will be like if they make no changes. Mere words don't seem to impress these guys."

Dahlia thought about it for a moment. "Have you seen Miss Piggy yet?" Dahlia told him.

"What is a Miss Piggy?" Grant laughed, looking dubious.

"Miss Piggy is a C-46 aircraft. She's called Miss Piggy because she was able to hold so much freight. Years ago she actually did transport pigs on board.

She was to fly from Churchill to Chesterfield Inlet but lost oil pressure in her left engine shortly after departing Churchill. She crashlanded, and Miss Piggy became a tourist attraction, sitting there gutted on the rocks."

"Interesting," he agreed. "But how does this teach the boys?"

"The load was probably too heavy. Later they speculated it wasn't properly checked. That's likely what caused the crash." She raised an eyebrow. "How would you like to be the guy who loaded that plane? A mistake like that—" She let it trail away.

"It could have cost lives," he finished, nodding. "I see where you're going," Grant said. "Being responsible in everything so you don't cost people their lives, doing your job in every detail, not sloughing off just to get a paycheck—it would be a good lesson for the boys." He checked his watch. "I'm supposed to meet with them in twenty minutes. Want to come?"

"You wouldn't mind?" she asked, thrilled to be included.

"Not at all. Are you done here?"

"I am. It'll be nice to have an excuse to go to Lives and see Arlen."

Grant was silent as they walked back to her vehicle. When they arrived, he stopped and laid his hand on her arm. Her skin began to tingle at his touch.

"I want to mention something, Dahlia. About Arlen."

The serious tone of his voice made Dahlia steel herself.

"Arlen's got a lot of pent-up emotions. He wants to lash out. You're making yourself a perfect target for his anger by being so available to him." Grant's eyes held hers.

"I just want to be his friend," she said, blushing under his scrutiny.

"Arlen may not be ready to be friends, with anybody." His gaze softened, chasing away the chill of the afternoon. "Dahlia, this kid—he's not in a place where he can appreciate that you're trying to help him. He's locked up in his own painful world. You might have to back off for a while."

"I care about him," she said stubbornly. "How can I not feel that?"

"I'm not saying don't care." Grant smiled. "Just protect yourself."

"How?" she demanded.

"Don't be so—" He searched for the right word. "Vulnerable," he said at last. "He's getting his kicks from seeing your disappointment when he slights you or ignores you. Don't focus on him alone. Treat him as one of the group and if he doesn't respond, ignore him."

Dahlia hated hearing those words and for a moment, she wanted to argue. But Grant was a counselor and part of her knew he was right. They got in her car and headed toward Lives.

"I don't want Arlen to hurt you," Grant said breaking the silence that had fallen between them. "But he seems to want to. For some reason I think hurting you helps him, maybe takes the focus off of what's really underneath all that pain."

"I'll try to be more blasé with him," she said at last. "But I'm not giving up. I still want to adopt him."

"I know, but—" Grant was obviously struggling with something. Finally, he said, "He has a mom, Dahlia."

Dahlia was surprised to hear this. She'd thought Arlen was all alone.

"She made him a ward of the court," Grant added.

"So he doesn't *really* have a family, and his mother obviously isn't meeting his needs," Dahlia argued. "So maybe I can be his refuge."

Grant frowned. He opened his mouth, but Dahlia cut him off.

"I *am* going to have this boy in my life. Somehow. And you can't talk me out of it."

Grant nodded, but his face grew very serious, as if he was deeply troubled by her words.

Everything Grant had said depressed her. But Arlen was exactly like her brother. He needed her and she was going to be there for him. She would not fail again. Grant made her feel as if her dream of adopting Arlen would never come true. And it *had* to. Because that was part of God's plan for her, that's why He'd laid this particular boy on her heart. She knew it just as she knew making the go-kart track was the task He'd given her to help the boys and prove herself strong.

When they pulled up to Lives, she stepped out of the truck and walked to the front door. She entered the building in front of Grant. All her apprehension melted at the sound of the boys' laughter and the twins' high-pitched squeals.

It was easy for Grant to warn her off—he had two amazing little girls in his life.

She had no one. But she would soon, somehow. She had to.

* * *

"How are you, Arlen?"

Grant gritted his teeth at the sound of Dahlia's ingratiating tone. Hadn't the woman heard anything he'd said? He held his breath, waiting for the boy's sour retort. Arlen didn't respond.

Grant stepped into the kitchen, wondering why. He caught his breath at the sight of Arlen seated at the table, with a twin on either side. He was folding paper into an airplane. A huge smile transformed his usually surly face. Grant caught his breath when Glory reached up to touch his cheek.

Don't hurt her, please don't hurt her.

But Arlen's smile only grew as he smoothed the mess of curls off her face. "Didn't you comb your hair this morning, Glory?" he said in a very tender voice.

"Daddy tried, but he's not very good at it."

Grant's face burned at this condemnation.

"She gets knots," Grace explained. "Daddy doesn't like hurting her so he bundles her hair up like that. But it never stays. Are you going to make me an airplane, too, Arlen?"

"Of course." The boy's grin made him look like a different kid. In seconds he made Grace's airplane and sent it zooming across the room. His grin disappeared when he saw Grant. "I'm not doing anything wrong," he said.

"No, you're not." Grant glanced around the room. "Where's Laurel?"

"Am I her keeper?" Arlen demanded.

"Arlen, make it fly again!" Grace called as she retrieved her plane.

"You got it." Arlen's surliness vanished. Then he looked at Grant. "Laurel's in her office, on the phone with someone named Teddy," he said in a more respectful voice.

"Dahlia, want to come find Laurel with me?" Grant didn't want her fawning over Arlen.

Dahlia nodded and left the room with him. "Arlen seems to have bonded with the twins."

"I noticed." Grant wasn't sure whether to be glad or worried. But he was pleased to see that the boy had a much softer side under that grumpiness. "Who is this Teddy he was talking about?"

"Teddy Stonechild. Kyle—have you met him? Lives' activities director?" She waited for his nod. "Kyle and his father used to own a guiding outfit. Teddy came to Churchill to go on a trip with them a long time ago and kept coming back. Now he stays longer because his son is taking over his hotel business in Vancouver."

"And he and Laurel are…?" He deliberately left the question hanging in the air.

"No one can quite figure out what's between them," Dahlia said with a smile. "They started out at each other's throats, but lately Teddy's always here when Laurel needs help, which seems to be quite a lot."

Laurel emerged from her office and stopped short. She glanced from Dahlia to Grant and arched a brow. "I hope you didn't mind me asking Arlen to watch the girls. He's got some kind of rapport with them. I thought it might be something we could build on."

"Good idea," Grant said, though he wasn't sure it was. Another thing about fatherhood that bugged him—there was no black and white. He stepped into the kitchen and stopped dead, astounded by what he saw in front of him.

"Don't we look nice, Daddy?" Grace said.

She turned so he could admire her perfectly French-braided hair. Glory's hair was the same but slightly off-side. Grant knew that was because she'd wiggled more than her sister.

"You both look very nice," he said, trying not to sound surprised. "Did Arlen do it for you?"

"Yes." Glory skipped toward him, took his hand on one side and Dahlia's on the other and swung herself. "He knows lots of ways to comb hair 'cause he used to do his sisters'."

Grant stared at his daughter. She'd learned more about this boy in the few minutes they'd been together than he'd managed in two sessions.

Arlen rose, looking everywhere but at them. "It was getting in the way when they were trying to color so I braided it."

"Thank you." Grant glanced at Dahlia, who looked as amazed as he did.

"Maybe you could show Daddy how to braid," Grace said, her hand tucked inside Arlen's.

"No." Arlen's cheeks turned red. He shook his head and sat back down. "Are we having a session or not?" he asked in his usual cranky tone.

"We are. I have something to talk to you about," Grant said, clearing his throat. "Then I'd like us all to go on a field trip."

Laurel called the other boys to join them. Grant began by speaking about mistakes that changed lives. Once he mentioned the crashed plane, it didn't take much persuading to get them excited to go see it. Soon Grant was driving toward Miss Piggy with Dahlia giving him directions. The twins sat belted in the backseat, and Laurel followed in the van with the boys.

"They really do look cute with those braids," Dahlia said in a soft voice. Grant wondered if she'd also noticed their shabby clothes.

"I tried to get Grace and Glory some new clothes at the northern store," he explained. "But they don't have anything the twins' size."

"They don't generally carry many clothes. Most people stock up for their kids in Thompson. It's cheaper. I might have an idea about that. Give me a couple of days, okay?"

Grant felt a rush of gratitude but ignored the urge he had to reach out and take her hand. He was going to ask about her idea when she directed him to pull over. They'd arrived at the site of a half-demolished plane rammed into a hill. He'd never seen anything like it.

"It's quite a sight, isn't it?" she asked.

To say the least. Grant acceded to the girls' demands to be freed of their seat belts. Worried about their safety as they gazed in awe at the metal body ripped open by the impact of the crash, he grabbed their hands, insisting they stay with him.

"It's easier if we go around this way." Dahlia pointed.

Grant followed her sure-footed steps over the slippery moss-covered rocks and remembered she'd said she taught gymnastics. As far as he could tell, Dahlia did everything well. A moment later she reached out a hand to Glory, and Grant couldn't help but enjoy the sight of this lovely woman looking after his daughter. He followed with Grace until they stood beside her.

"Go ahead and look around," Dahlia urged the boys who'd just arrived. That blazing smile spread across her face as she turned to Grant. "I can see all of you are going to need some inspection time. I'll watch the girls while you look."

Grant accepted the offer, realizing that he was perfectly comfortable leaving the twins in Dahlia's capable hands. It was an unfamiliar feeling, being comfortable leaving them with someone else. Of course, Dahlia was… Dahlia. She was special.

He shook off the thought and went to inspect the craft with the boys.

When they'd finished, Grant sat on a rock at the top of the hill and waited until, one by one, the boys flopped down around him. The light breeze off the bay kept the afternoon comfortable. It was the perfect setting for teaching, making him think of similar settings in which Jesus had often taught.

"The sign doesn't say much about why the plane crashed," Rod said with a frown. "I looked it up at the museum once. The cargo was too heavy and the grounds crew probably didn't check the weight."

"Bad mistake, huh?" Grant said. "Nobody died, but they could have."

Arlen sneered. "What were they—dummies?"

"I doubt it," Grant said. "It's more likely they had a busy day, they'd done it thousands of times and got careless. Could happen to anyone, right?"

"Not hardly," Arlen rushed in. "A job like that, you have to know what you're doing. You don't fake it."

Grant looked at Dahlia. She smiled, and he knew she was thinking that this was exactly the opportunity he'd wanted. He smiled back, trying to ignore the fact that something was happening between them, that he felt a connection to her that was undeniable. It concerned him.

But he decided he'd deal with that later. For now, it just felt good to have her on his side.

Dahlia sat beside the twins, spellbound by Grant's voice as he led the boys toward self-evaluation. He laughed and joked, teasing and gently encouraging until they considered their own situations and came up with changes they could make to improve their futures.

She couldn't believe the difference in Grant. This incredible coach seemed miles from the distant, self-effacing, almost helpless father she'd seen with the twins. He didn't falter, didn't question himself and didn't hesitate. Even Grace and Glory seemed to understand that this was a precious moment of learning for the Lives boys. They sat quietly, peeling moss from the rocks and piling it in small mounds.

"Everything, guys," Grant paused to emphasize his point. "Every single thing you do has consequences. You may not see them right away. But there is a result and it won't always be what you want or expect. That's why you have to be so careful about your choices."

All of the boys seemed to ponder Grant's words, except Arlen.

"What do you know about our choices?" the boy sneered.

"Everybody has to make them. It's part of life." Grant smiled at him. "So think carefully, because you are a result of the choices you make. Change your choices, change your life." Seconds passed and no one spoke. Grant rose, and brushed off his pants.

"If you're ready, guys, I think we should head back to Lives," Laurel said.

As the boys climbed into the van, Dahlia pulled Laurel aside.

"Can I present my go-kart idea after they've eaten?" she asked.

"Sure. I'll leave it to you to bring up the subject when you're ready."

Dahlia was on tenterhooks during the drive back to Lives. This was going to be a lot of work and she could only hope the boys wouldn't give up part way through the project. When they arrived, Grant gave her a sidelong look as the girls preceded him into Lives. He reached out and touched her arm.

"Remember, I'm here to help," he murmured.

"Thank you." His touch and those gentle words silenced the fear inside her.

This was what she was supposed to do.

The boys were quieter during dinner, obviously mulling over Grant's words. Arlen was the first to rise to leave the table.

"Can you wait a minute, please, Arlen? I want to talk to you all about something."

"Not another lecture," Arlen muttered.

"Not at all," she said, smiling at him even though her heart ached when he rolled his eyes. "It's an idea I have. I want to know if you're interested."

Slowly, she laid out her plan in clear terms, her heart filling with hope when the boys began to chat excitedly. Only Arlen looked unimpressed.

"Let me get this straight," he said, glaring at her with dark eyes. "You want us to slave out there in the elements to make this thing for you—"

"Oh, no," Dahlia interrupted with a firm shake of her head. "It's not for me. It's for you. All of you will be able to use the go-kart track when it's finished."

"How would we do this?" Rod asked, shooting Arlen a glance that Dahlia interpreted as "chill out."

"Here's my plan," Dahlia began. "First we'd have to clear the road. There are a few places where we'll need to do some minor repair on the asphalt." A rush of excitement filled her when heads began nodding. "Then we'll need to collect tires to put around the perimeter of the track."

"I've seen go-kart tracks where they paint the tires. Maybe red and black?" Kris said. When Arlen glared at him, Kris quickly bowed his head.

"The colors will be up to you boys to choose together," she told them, encouraged by the looks on their faces. "I've found some go-karts, but they need work. We'll have to find someone in town who can help with the mechanical stuff."

"My dad's a mechanic. I grew up helping in his shop," David said. "I helped rebuild motors lots of times."

"That's a valuable skill." Grant's gaze locked with Dahlia's, and the smile on his face made her skin tingle. She focused on the six boys, delighted by their response. *Thank you, Lord.*

"Sounds like a lot of work," Arlen said in an obnoxious tone.

"Yes, it does," Laurel spoke up. "That's why each of you needs to decide whether or not you want to be part of this. I don't think it's fair to ask Dahlia to organize everything and then have us quit when it gets hard. If we say 'yes,' we're in it—together—until it's finished."

The boys stared at each other.

"Wouldn't the kids at school be impressed?" Rod asked, a tiny grin twitching at the corner of his mouth.

When Dahlia looked at Grant, he winked. Inside, a tiny ember flamed to life. What an encourager he was.

"Maybe when it's finished, you could invite some of the school kids out to see what you've created," Grant suggested.

"Like they'd come," Arlen said.

"Oh, I'm pretty sure they'd come." Grant grinned. "They wouldn't be able to help themselves. After all, how many go-kart tracks are there in Churchill?"

"I'm in," Marten said to Dahlia. The other boys followed his lead—all but Arlen, who stayed silent.

"I'm so glad you're enthusiastic," she said with a smile. "But I want you to think about this until Monday. Then we'll take a vote. Okay?"

"I think that's a good idea." Laurel glanced around the table. "Any other thoughts?"

"Why don't we take a look at the road now?" Grant suggested. "That way, we'll all have a better idea of what will be involved in making this work."

Dahlia followed them outside, thrilled by their excitement yet still troubled.

"You've really engaged them with this plan of yours," Grant said, walking beside her as the twins surged ahead on either side of Arlen.

"All except Arlen," she reminded him. She tried to hide her hurt.

"Dahlia." Grant reached for her arm to stop her. "Give it time. Something in his past hurt him deeply. It won't heal overnight."

"I know." Wistfully, she lifted her head to search him out and faltered to a stop. Without thinking, she grabbed Grant's hand and squeezed it. "Look!" she whispered.

In front of them, the twins had each taken one of Arlen's hands and were dragging him to see a bird sitting on a boulder. He burst out laughing at something they said, but then his laughter died away. He murmured something to the girls and the three of them crouched down to study the obviously injured animal.

Dahlia's heart squeezed as the embittered boy gathered the tiny bird into his hands. Gently, tenderly he cradled it, showing the twins how to soothe it.

"I never knew he cared about birds," she whispered. Only then did Dahlia realize Grant's fingers had curled around hers, warming her hand.

And for the life of her, she could not make herself break contact.

Dahlia was supposed to be strong, in control. She had no desire to open her heart to another man after what had happened with Charles. But she couldn't deny that it felt good to relax in Grant's protective clasp, just for a moment.

He was becoming a great friend, but that's all it was. And that's all it could ever be. No matter how nice it felt to hold his hand.

Chapter Five

Grant stared as Dahlia lugged bags brimming with clothes inside his house. He'd been thinking about her all day and now here she was.

"What is all this?"

"Stuff for the girls." Dahlia chuckled as the twins raced over and threw their arms around her legs. "Want to have a fashion show?" she asked them.

The twins were delighted even though Grant was fairly certain they had no idea what a fashion show was. After explaining the concept to them, Dahlia ordered him to sit on the sofa and wait as she ushered the twins into their rooms.

After a few minutes of giggles followed by Dahlia's whispers to hush, Grant rose and poured himself a cup of coffee. He returned to his seat thinking about the unusual woman who kept appearing in his life. Not that he objected. Far from it.

In the three weeks since he'd arrived in Churchill, Dahlia had been his lifesaver many times. She'd introduced him to countless locals, brought over casseroles for dinner and helped him get a feel for the small town and for how things ran at Lives where he often ran into her.

"Ta da! Look, Daddy!" Glory pranced in front of him clad in a cute pair of blue jeans and a matching denim shirt. "Aren't they pretty?"

"Yes, they are," he agreed, surprised by how well the items fit. "You look lovely. And so do you," he said to Grace, who strutted out in a red jumper dress with a white blouse. "Where did you get these?" he asked Dahlia, who stood watching from the bedroom door, her face glowing.

"I made them," she said breezily, as if it were a simple thing.

"You made them?" Grant asked, incredulous.

Dahlia laughed at his surprise. "I love to sew, especially for kids. Come on, girls, time to change outfits."

The twins squealed as they scurried back into their bedroom.

Dahlia lingered, her smile warming him inside. "Don't move," she said.

Again and again, the twins modeled their

new clothing, including Sunday dresses, school clothes and rough-and-tumble play outfits. There were also two winter coats, one a dark emerald-green, the other a softer shade of a pretty jade tone.

"Surely you didn't make the coats?" Grant said, watching the twins snuggle their faces into the fuzzy trim around the hoods. When Dahlia didn't answer, he searched her face.

"No," she finally admitted. "I ordered them online. They were on sale," she said defensively.

He was embarrassed. He'd known he had to get the girls new coats, but he just hadn't gotten around to ordering them. Not the kind of thing a proper father would do, he now realized. Clothing your kids was as basic as feeding them.

"I'll reimburse you."

"That's not necessary."

"I insist. For the fabric also," he added. She must have spent a lot on the buttons and trim that created the individual touches the girls loved.

"Grant, please don't," Dahlia begged. Her eyes glistened as she watched Glory and Grace trade jackets. "Making these few things has brought me so much joy."

He smiled when he saw a little heart-trimmed pocket on the backside of Glory's jeans. "This is more, much more, than any friend would do."

"I guess that depends on your friends." Her incredible eyes held his for a long moment. "I had such fun. Please."

Grant knew he couldn't push it. He couldn't stand to see those expressive eyes lose their glow.

When and how had Dahlia's happiness come to matter so much?

"Okay, Dahlia. I insist on repaying you for the coats, but for the rest—thank you," he said, hoping she realized how much her gift meant to him.

"Thank *you*." Dahlia smiled, and for a moment, Grant felt the urge to do whatever it took to keep that smile on her beautiful face.

She turned back to the twins and hunkered down to their level. "Can I ask you to do something for me?"

"Sure," Glory chirped. "You're our friend. We help our friends."

"Yes, we do." Dahlia tossed Grant a sideways glance, her lips twitching with amusement. "If someone asks you about your new clothes, could you just say a friend gave them to you? Don't say my name," Dahlia clarified. "Just say a friend."

"You don't want anyone to know." Grace frowned.

"How come?" Glory demanded.

"Because I don't want anyone to feel bad that I didn't make something special for them, too. I'm very busy right now. Your daddy and I are working on a project with the boys at Lives."

"Is it for Arlen?" Glory's serious blue eyes looked from Dahlia to Grant.

"Yes, for Arlen," Dahlia admitted. "And the other boys, too."

Grace's face suddenly fell. "Arlen's sad inside."

"What do you mean, Grace?" Grant knelt next to Dahlia to get closer to his daughter. "Did he tell you that?"

Grace shook her red-gold head. "I can feel it. Here," she said, laying a hand over her heart.

Grant looked at Dahlia, who was gazing at Grace in amazement.

"You have the kind of heart that sees pain inside a person, sweetie." Dahlia caressed Grace's cheek. "It's wonderful that you want Arlen to be happy. I do, too." She rose. "Now I need to ask your dad something in private. Maybe you can go hang up your new coats."

But Glory had another question. "Did you sew anything for Daddy?" she asked. "Sometimes his shirts don't have buttons."

"I'm sorry about that." Dahlia grinned at him, her eyes dancing. "Maybe I'll have to show him how to sew."

"I already know how to sew on a button, thanks." Grant's cheeks burned. "I'll get around to it when I get time. Go hang up your coats now."

Glory left, frowning. She and Grace were whispering as they went into their room. Grant heard laughter and turned. Dahlia's shoulders were shaking.

"Go ahead, laugh," he said. "It seems there's no end to the humiliation those two are willing to subject me to."

"I think it's adorable that they want me to make sure you're cared for. They're very thoughtful girls. You should be proud," Dahlia said.

"That was their mother's doing. I'm just the stand-in—"

"I really wish you'd stop doing that."

"Doing what?" he asked.

"Putting yourself down. You've kept them fed, healthy and housed. Why do you always negate that?" Dahlia shook her head, her glorious curls dancing. "You give them love. They need that far more than new clothes or a new winter coat."

"I do love them," he said quietly. "But I'm not sure they know it. When I was a kid—well, hugs, affection—that wasn't part of my life."

"Grant." Dahlia fingers closed over his. "Glory

and Grace know you love them and it has nothing to do with whether or not you hug them. You heard what they said about Arlen. Those two can see into a person's heart. They can see into yours."

"I hope so," he said dubiously. "Was that what you wanted to talk to me about?"

"No." She got a strange look on her face. "I, uh, need your help."

"My help?" He stared at her in confusion. "With what?"

She took a deep breath.

"Okay, this is embarrassing." Dahlia inhaled, looked him straight in the eye and let the story out in a rush of words. "There's this guy, a nice guy, called Eddie Smart. He works up north in the mines. Every time he's about to leave town he asks me out and I always put him off and say, 'Next time.' Well, he wants next time to be tonight. He called to ask me to go with him to the fall supper. I didn't want to go with him, but I couldn't think of a good excuse so—well, I told him I was going with you and the twins."

Grant was so surprised he didn't know what to say. He'd never seen Dahlia so rattled.

"Eddie's not a bad guy, he just wants there to be something between us. There isn't, and there won't be," she said emphatically. "But I don't want to hurt him or to keep his hopes up. So will you go?"

"To this fall supper?" Grant finished. "With you?"

"Yes. One of the local service groups holds it every year to raise funds," she explained. "When a family has to take a child to Winnipeg for treatment, this group helps cover the cost of the parents' flights and lodging so they can be with their child."

"Nice." Grant noticed her pink cheeks. He almost wanted to keep her in suspense just to see how pink they'd get so he didn't accept her invitation. Yet.

"I'll pay for your supper and the twins'," she assured him, the emerald tones in her eyes blazing. "In fact I already bought the tickets. I like to support local events."

"I see." Grant nodded, trying to keep a straight face. "But what about this Eddie? Am I going to have to fend him off?"

Dahlia laughed, a sound that Grant was discovering he liked a lot.

"No, no. That won't be an issue." The gold flecks in her eyes danced when she gave him a secretive little smile. "I've arranged for someone else to sit with him. Marni Parker, who owns Polar Bear Pizza, thinks Eddie's the best thing since sliced bread. But he doesn't notice her because he's got these silly daydreams about me." She blushed again, a beautiful rose tone that washed over her entire face and neck. "I thought if he saw me with you and Marni was there to console him…"

She had a finger in every pot. Sweet, conniving Dahlia Wheatley. The woman amazed him.

"You're asking me to share a meal I don't have to cook? How could I say no?" Grant chuckled when Dahlia let out a sigh of relief. "But aren't you worried that people will talk about us?" he teased.

Dahlia shook her head. "I think most people in town realize I'm not interested in getting married. I'm too independent."

Grant felt a rush of disappointment, and told himself he was being silly for all sorts of reasons. He wasn't interested in marriage either, not after everything that had happened. Plus, he barely knew Dahlia—why should her opinions about marriage have any effect on him?

The hall was decorated in a fall theme and filled with people, most of whom Grant didn't know. But Dahlia smiled at everyone. She introduced him to so many people that Grant gave up trying to remember their names.

"It's our turn to sit down," Dahlia said just

as the twins began to fidget, a sure sign they were hungry.

They had just taken their seats when a brown-haired man pushed his way through the crowd and stopped in front of Dahlia.

"Hi there," he said, gazing at her with a sheepish look.

"Oh, hi, Eddie," Dahlia said graciously. "How are you?"

They exchanged pleasantries; then she introduced him to Grant and the girls. Grant could understand Eddie's injured look—it probably wasn't easy to realize you'd lost a chance with a woman like Dahlia.

"I have the other tickets but the numbers aren't together," Dahlia explained. "But I thought you might enjoy eating with Marni. She's just back from her trip to Banff. I know how you love that park, Eddie."

Grant watched in awe as Dahlia beckoned Marni over and facilitated a conversation between the two. Soon, the couple left to claim seats on the far side of the room. Grant chuckled.

"Nicely done, Ms. Matchmaker," he said.

"Oh, shush," she said with a grin. "Pastor Rick will say grace for everyone and then we can go up and fill our plates."

That was when Grant realized that he'd have

to battle with the twins over their food selections in front of the entire town. Everyone would hear the twins' protest about food that wasn't like their mother's, and he'd look like an idiot.

But after grace, Dahlia led the girls through the buffet line, adding a bit of this, a spoonful of that to their plates. She deftly handled their questions, assuring them that roast turkey was every bit as good as tofu.

Grant got so caught up in Dahlia's handling of the situation that he paid little attention to his own plate until they returned to their table.

"You really like Brussels sprouts, huh?" Dahlia asked, gazing at his plate.

He looked down, dismayed by the huge serving on his plate. When he glanced up, Dahlia's eyebrows rose. "I won't tease you about Eddie if you don't ask about my Brussels sprouts," he told her.

"Deal!" She grinned, then tucked into her food. "Isn't this great? I love fall suppers."

"There's more than one?" he asked.

"There are four. One is all fish. Deep-fried, battered, baked or smoked. You'll love it." She tweaked Grace's nose. "So will you."

Grace smiled happily as if she'd never had an issue with food.

"They always have lots of leftovers," Dahlia said. "For a five dollar donation you get a take-out container with enough food for another meal. You order them from Jeff, the guy with the green apron and the funny hat."

When Jeff came near, Grant ordered several containers, minus the Brussels sprouts.

"Six?" Dahlia said, green eyes wide.

"Six meals I won't have to cook. Besides," he murmured with a sideways look. "I already know the twins like them."

"And your choice of vegetable?" Dahlia teased.

"Brussels sprouts don't refreeze well. Corn does."

"Right. That's the reason." She giggled. Her smile grew when a young couple stopped by to chat.

Grant took the twins to the pie table, leaving Dahlia to chat with her friends. Grace insisted lemon was Dahlia's favorite so he brought back a piece for her.

"Thank you," she said, savoring her first taste. "But you shouldn't have left. I would have introduced you to Elena and Higgins. They're just back from their honeymoon."

"Your work?" he asked, tongue in cheek.

"I might have introduced them," she said, tongue in cheek. "They did the rest themselves."

"Higgins is a miner, too?"

"There are a number of miners who live here

but work up north. It's convenient for them to fly in and out of Churchill."

"I'm guessing Eddie isn't the only one who's asked you out."

Blushing but not answering him, Dahlia turned to the twins and begged them for a taste of their pie. Her eyes twinkled when she noticed his uneaten slice.

"You don't like pumpkin pie?" Dahlia reached out as if to take it and burst out laughing when he pulled it away. "Your daddy has a sweet tooth, I think," she whispered to Grace.

"Can I see it, Daddy?" Grace wiggled closer to him, trying to look into his mouth.

Once again, Dahlia hooted with laughter. Grant had never known anyone who laughed so much. It was a lovely sound.

"There are kids' games in that room over there," she told him. "We could take our coffee along while Grace and Glory try the fishing pond." Dahlia waited for his nod, then rose and led the way. At first, the girls held back, but once Dahlia showed them how the game worked, they were fully involved. "So cute," she murmured.

So was she, Grant thought. Cute and generous and amazing with the twins.

"Dahlia, is this the man you were telling me about?" A diminutive, silver-haired woman nudged her way between Grant and Dahlia. She smiled and thrust out an arthritic hand. "Hello. I'm Lucy Clow. This is my husband, Hector. I understand you need someone to watch the twins after school. I'd love to help."

For a moment, Grant couldn't say a word. Dahlia had done this, probably heard him tell Laurel his worry about leaving the girls in so many after-school programs. How had she known he'd hoped to find exactly this type of woman to watch the girls?

No wonder the miners of Churchill were all interested in Dahlia.

She was, quite simply, amazing.

Grant thought back to all the times he'd thought that Dahlia would be a wonderful mother, and he began to wonder if perhaps the marriage-of-convenience idea he'd first considered on the train that day wasn't so crazy after all.

Dahlia couldn't figure out why Grant suddenly seemed tongue-tied. She shared town news with Hector and Lucy for a moment. Finally she nudged Grant's arm and he seemed to snap back.

In a matter of minutes he and Lucy had arranged everything, he'd introduced her to the twins and they'd fawned all over the smiling grandmother. Beaming, Lucy fluttered a wave before she and Hector left.

"You don't want to check out Lucy before hiring her?" Dahlia asked.

"You and Laurel both talk about her so glowingly. That's good enough for me." The twins asked if they could go back to the games, and Grant nodded. "She mentions God a lot. Is she religious?"

"Lucy's faith is an intimate part of her life. In fact, she and Hector used to be missionaries to the Inuit. God is important to her."

"Maybe she's the answer to my prayer." Grant blinked as if startled he'd admitted that.

"How's that?"

"I need someone who'll be able to teach the twins Eva's faith," he said in a thoughtful tone. "Lucy sounds like the perfect woman to do that."

"I see," she said, but it was clear she didn't.

"You're probably thinking that's something I should do," he guessed. "But I can't. I don't have that rock-solid faith in God that Eva had. I was trying to learn before she died…" Grant trailed off and was silent for a moment. "Anyway, it sounds as if Lucy's faith is strong, like Eva's was."

"Lucy's faith *is* strong," assured Dahlia. "But faith is a learning curve for all of us." She smiled, feeling the wryness of her statement. "I'm going through a faith test myself."

The moment she said it, Dahlia wished she hadn't. Grant knew too much about her already. He drew her confidence so that she blurted out things she shouldn't, things she'd usually kept bottled up inside.

"Arlen?" Grant guessed. She nodded. "You're trying to have faith that you'll be able to adopt him?"

"I'm trying to trust that God will direct things," she corrected quietly. "But I'm also trying to be mindful that His way isn't always mine."

His gaze rested on her, a troubled cloud in its depths.

"I wouldn't want you to get hurt, Dahlia. Arlen has a lot of anger buried inside, though I think most of it is directed at himself."

Dahlia wanted to press Grant, but she could tell that he wouldn't reveal details. It was clear he felt his responsibility to the boys very keenly. So she changed the subject.

"See that group of men over there?" When he nodded, she smiled. "They're dads who bring their kids to my gymnastic class on Thursday evenings. It's for parents and kids. You're welcome to join us. I think the twins would love it, too."

Grant glanced from the men to the girls and back to her.

"They're nice guys," she assured him. "Want me to introduce you?"

"Thanks, but I'll need to think it over and see if I have time," he said.

"Is that the real reason?" she asked softly.

"What do you mean?"

"Churchill is a small town, but most of us try not to judge. Every one of us has problems," Dahlia told him. "If we can help our neighbor, we do. That's what makes this such a wonderful community. Join us, Grant. A little fun among friends might be just what you and the girls need."

By the end of the evening, Grant felt a lot more comfortable mixing with the community, and that was due to Dahlia. She laughed with everyone, drawing him into the conversation so he could join their discussions. When the twins ran up and threw their arms around her, Dahlia's face glowed with pride and love and Grant knew she'd make a wonderful mother.

He was pretty sure she'd take the cake in the "wife" division, too, but he'd think about that some other time. Tonight he'd decided to ask her for her help, even though he was positive it wasn't the kind of help she had in mind. When they were finally alone he touched her arm to get her attention.

"Dahlia, would you give me a hand getting the twins home and in bed? After that, I'd like to ask you something." For a moment he thought she could see inside him, that she had a clear view of all his insecurities. Then the warmth of her smile washed over him.

"I'd love to and you can ask me whatever you want." Her grin blazed; her laughter rang to the ceiling. Joy spilled from Dahlia Wheatley like an artesian well.

To have that in his life, in the twins' lives, would be about the best answer to prayer God could give him.

Now all Grant had to do was figure out the right way to ask Dahlia to marry him.

Chapter Six

"You're so blessed." Dahlia collapsed onto Grant's sofa with a sigh. "Those girls of yours are a delight. I haven't had so much fun in a long time."

"Well, they absolutely adore you."

"The feeling is mutual." Dahlia took a sip of her tea, noticing that Grant seemed preoccupied. When he sat down across from her, his face was very serious. A frisson of worry tickled up her spine. "Is anything wrong?"

"No. Not wrong." He kept watching her. "It's— Uh, I wanted to ask you something."

"Go ahead." She shifted under the intense scrutiny of those gray eyes, especially when she realized *he* was nervous, too. "What is it?" she demanded when the silence stretched too long.

Grant inhaled then coughed. He set down his cup and took one of her hands. An eerie sense of déjà vu struck Dahlia, but she couldn't imagine why. Until he spoke.

"Dahlia, do you think—that is, would you consider...marrying me?"

She pulled her hand away and reared back. "Are you joking?"

"Not at all," Grant said, his voice too calm.

"But—why?" A thousand things rushed through her head, primarily that she'd jumped from the frying pan with Eddie into the fire with Grant. "I mean, I... We're...not in love, so..." She let it trail away, waiting for him to explain.

"I'm not talking about a regular marriage," he explained. "You've already told me, in no uncertain terms, that you're not interested in that. I'm talking about a different kind of marriage."

"Grant, it might be better—" The words snagged in her throat as his hands closed around hers.

"Please, give me a chance to explain. Please?" he asked. Sincerity blazed from his eyes and begged her to hear him out. "I haven't told you much about my childhood. Let's just say it wasn't pleasant. My father cared only for himself. The only tenderness I ever knew came from my mother and she left when I was quite young."

"I'm sorry," she whispered, tears forming on her lashes at the thought of a young Grant suffering such a loss.

"It was ugly, but I survived. I made my own way, went to school, got a job and met someone. The relationship turned into disaster. She wanted me to love her and I couldn't give what I couldn't feel," he said. "I didn't know how to handle her emotional demands so it ended."

"That must have been hard."

"It was," he agreed, his lips pinched tight. "I moved, started over. When it happened the second time, I figured that if I got counseling, I could change things." He gave her a self-mocking smile. "I finally grasped that because of my past, I'm not able to get past my—" He paused, searching for the right word. "I guess you'd say inhibitions. I decided to stay single. I never wanted to put a child through what I went through."

Dahlia didn't understand. "But you did get married."

"To Eva." His smile was genuine. "Yes."

"So?"

"Eva persuaded me that I needed the right teacher to show me how to be a husband and a father. She insisted *she* was that teacher, that she could help me change." Grant met her eyes. "And something did change. I had never believed that I could be a husband and a father, but with Eva, because I loved her, I started to believe that I could. But then she died and left the girls in my care, and I realized that I needed more than belief to be a good father. I needed knowledge and experience, neither of which I had."

"But you've figured it out now," Dahlia said.

"No, I haven't. Every morning I wake up terrified I'm missing something that will ruin their lives. And every day I make some stupid mistake that makes them cry." He looked up. "You've come to our rescue so many times. You always know exactly what to do. So I thought, you want someone to love, that's why you're trying so hard to reach Arlen. And here are two little girls who adore you, desperately needing a mom."

"Grant—I can't," she sputtered, searching for a way to make him understand.

"I wouldn't place any demands on you. It would be for the twins' sake, so that they could grow up happy and safe, knowing they are secure."

He made it sound so *sensible,* so easy. But Dahlia couldn't be drawn in to his plan.

"You're patient and tender and kind. You'd be an amazing mom, Dahlia."

His sweet words revived that inner longing to shower her love on someone, to build that strong, nurturing bond with another human. And yet—

"I can't marry you, Grant. You're a great guy, and I think you're an awesome dad no matter how many mistakes you make. You don't need me or anyone else. You're doing an amazing job."

"Dahlia," he said, peering into her eyes. "Nothing would have to change."

"Grant, no." She shook her head. "Listen. You think you need me, but you don't. You're learning every day, and the girls love you so much. You'll find your way, I promise. Besides, marriage isn't part of my plans."

"You keep saying that. Why?" Grant leaned back, his gaze intent as he studied her.

He'd bared his soul to her. The least she could do was return the favor.

"I told you I was once engaged," she began.

"Yes. To Charles, wasn't it?"

"So you understand why I'm not looking to get involved again." Dahlia lifted her gaze and saw Grant shaking his head.

"Not all men are like Charles," he said in that calm manner of his.

"It wasn't just Charles's betrayal." She exhaled. "Do you really need to hear this?"

"Yes. Please?" Grant sat there, quietly, patiently waiting for her to share.

Dahlia closed her eyes and the past filled her mind.

"I went on a mission trip to Haiti before my

last semester at university. It helped me understand so many things. I'd been sheltered and protected for so long, I'd lost sight of who I was, of my purpose. But in Haiti I saw these very poor people, some of whom had lost everything, and they were happy, truly happy."

"So you decided to change your life," he finished for her.

Maybe he could understand after all.

"Yes. I came home full of possibilities. One by one, they were crushed. My parents, Charles, my work. When Granny Bev died, I finally saw that if I married Charles I'd never be free. I'd always be sickly Dahlia to them. I knew that if I didn't leave, I'd begin to believe it about myself."

"So you came here and started your store."

"Yes." She sighed. "Now I feel I'm finally regaining my personal power. I'm proving to myself, and to my parents, if they care enough to find out, that I am strong, capable and competent. And I'm able to give back the way I want."

"Marrying me would put you back in the box?" Grant tented his fingers as he waited for her response.

"Marriage, period. Because that's part of what marriage, of what any partnership, is. No matter how equal you want things to be, there has to be one voice that's stronger, one person who prevails. Right now, *I* have to be that person in my life."

"That's something a lot of people don't figure out until it's too late," Grant agreed in a soft voice.

"So you understand." Anxious to make sure there was no misunderstanding, Dahlia said, "If I thought God wanted me to marry, if I felt He'd chosen someone for me, I would rethink my position. But that's not the case. You want a marriage of convenience."

"I want a mother for the girls, someone who will cover all the gaffes I make so I don't ruin their lives."

Grant didn't pretend romance. She liked his honesty.

"But there's no guarantee a wife would do that," Dahlia warned. "Besides, you're in control of their happiness now. Your past is over. You're the best parent they could have right now."

"I wish I were as certain," he said. Suddenly a speculative glow filled his gaze. "But maybe you can help me another way, Dahlia."

"Such as?" she asked uncertainly.

"You put couples together. Eddie and Marni. Higgins and Elena." As Grant's gaze met hers, warning lights flashed deep inside Dahlia. "Maybe you can find me a wife."

Dahlia sagged against the sofa back, seeking its support. How had she gotten herself into this?

"You know everyone in town and you know the twins. You must know who would be the most suitable candidate."

Some sixth sense warned her to run, yet Grant's shining gray eyes told her he was utterly sincere. She had to hear him out.

"Please, Dahlia, find me a wife."

She stared at him in shock, surprised to feel a flicker of envy pinch her heart. But how could she possibly be jealous of someone he didn't even know when she'd just refused his marriage proposal?

Grant couldn't remember the last time he'd felt so hopeful. Enlisting Dahlia's help was genius. *If* she agreed. He waited as a myriad of expressions chased across her face. Shock, of course, bewilderment, confusion, but then Dahlia seemed to consider his request.

"I won't put any demands on them except concerning the twins," he promised.

"But you want to avoid love?" Her scrutiny and especially the disbelief on her face irritated him. "The women around here are my friends, Grant. Most of them *want* love in their lives. They're looking for the fairy tale of happily-ever-after."

"Then don't introduce me to them," he said flatly. Dahlia seemed baffled.

"I guess."

"Something else is holding you back. What is it?"

"If I do this and something goes wrong, you'll blame me." She lifted her troubled gaze to meet his. "I like you, Grant. I don't want something to interfere with our friendship."

"I promise it won't." He meant it. Dahlia had become a good friend. He couldn't jeopardize that. "Just think about it. And, of course, if you don't want to do it, we'll still work together on the Lives project."

"Thank you." Relief filled her hazel eyes. Dahlia rose. "I must get home. I've got accounts to go over. Thanks for coming with me tonight."

"I enjoyed it." He grinned. "And my freezer's stocked up, too."

"Don't pretend you can't cook," she chided. "Glory told me all about that casserole you made. It sounded delicious."

"I can cook some things. What I haven't been able to master are Eva's recipes. They never turn out edible."

"Then don't make them anymore." She tilted her head to one side.

"But she was adamant the twins eat healthy food," he argued.

"There are lots of healthy recipes on the internet. Check them out." Her suggestion made him feel foolish.

"I know, but—" He sighed. "Eva had a system. I'm trying to honor that."

"Grant." Dahlia almost touched his arm but then quickly drew her hand back, leaving Grant to wonder what had stopped her. "You're striving to be both mom and dad to your kids," she continued. "That has to be frustrating. Besides, I doubt you have the time to master her system."

"No," he admitted ruefully. "I don't. But it was important to her."

"More important than the twins themselves?"

He hadn't thought of it that way. Still, guilt rose.

"But Eva would want—"

"—you to do your very best for her girls," Dahlia finished. "Wouldn't she?"

Grant slowly nodded.

"Stop beating yourself up. Eva wouldn't have wanted you to feel guilty for doing things differently," Dahlia insisted. "In fact, I'm sure she expected you would."

Eva hadn't been perfect and neither was he. She'd understand. A sense of relief washed through him thanks to the delicate-looking but tough woman in front of him. "You've made me see things from a new perspective. I appreciate that," Grant said. "So will you consider helping me, Dahlia?"

"Find a wife?" She studied him. "I have to pray about it, and you should, too."

"I will," he promised.

"Bring the girls to my gymnastics class. If you want to meet women that's a good place to go."

"I didn't exactly say I wanted to—" He loved it when she teased him.

He said good-night when she left, locked the door, cleaned up their tea things and then sat down to mull over the evening. A glow of hope flickered inside. Maybe soon he'd have someone to help with the twins.

Dahlia had told him to pray about it so Grant bowed his head and began to pray. But the funny thing was, whenever he tried to visualize a new mom for Glory and Grace, it was Dahlia's face he saw.

Chapter Seven

Dahlia adored her gymnastics students.

Full of hope and potential, they were willing to push themselves to achieve, and they were an inspiration to Dahlia. They also seemed to be inspiring Grace and Glory, who were having a great time.

Having not seen Grant for a week, Dahlia had felt a bump of satisfaction when he'd walked through the doors with Glory and Grace. She'd tried to ignore the question that buzzed in her head. *Was Grant here to meet a woman?*

"I'll have to spend some time showing our two newbies and their dad the ropes," she told Rod, whom she'd hired as an assistant. "Can you keep the others busy running through their paces?"

"Sure." He immediately called the group to order and began the opening routine.

"Hi. Glad you came," Dahlia said, smiling at Grant after she'd hugged the twins.

"Thanks. So, I guess I come back in an hour?" He met her gaze.

"What? No!" She laughed. "Parents are required to stay and pitch in."

Grant glanced at the girls, then back at her. "Pitch in?"

"Yes." She raised one eyebrow. "Is that an issue?"

It seemed eons passed before he responded. "It's fine."

"Great." Dahlia chuckled at the pained look on his face. "You can put your jackets over there if you like." Then she directed them to the beginner group. "Okay, folks, let's finish stretching."

Dahlia led everyone through the opening routine sequences, proud of the kids as they moved easily from station to station. She asked parents to stay partly to give those who were employed away from Churchill precious sharing moments with their kids.

Grant and the twins mimicked everyone else as they learned the routines. By break time, everyone was smiling, including Grant.

"Is everything okay?" she asked him. He nodded. She turned to the girls. "Are you having fun?" Their grins said it all. "There's coffee over there for your dad and juice boxes for you. The cookies are for everyone."

"Cookies?" The twins' expressive eyes begged Grant for permission. He nodded and they dashed away. He and Dahlia followed.

"I've been meaning to call you about the track," she said hopefully. "I have some time Saturday afternoon, after four. Would you be available to help?"

"That's good for me." He accepted the coffee she handed him. "What needs doing?"

"Weeding. But that should go quickly since Laurel's bringing the boys."

"Then what?" Grant asked.

"I've received a prefab hut, which I thought could be a starting point for the go-karts. It needs to be assembled." She saw his doubt. "It's not hard, but it takes several people."

Grant agreed, but Dahlia noticed that his attention was on a woman in a red shirt chatting with Grace.

"That's Enid Thompson," Dahlia offered. "She's a teacher. Her son, Ben, is the blond boy who's bouncing all over the place." Dahlia studied Grant. "Have you met her?"

"No," he said.

"She's single. Her husband divorced her and left Churchill just after Ben was born. She teaches fourth grade."

"Single, huh?" Grant sipped his coffee thoughtfully.

"Would you like me to introduce you?" A twinge of jealousy caught Dahlia off guard. She suppressed her dislike at the thought of Grant being interested in Enid. But he *was* looking for a mother for the twins, and Enid had experience with motherhood. "Enid," she called. "I'd like you to meet someone."

Enid was smiling at something Glory had said when she looked up. Dahlia had never thought about Enid's looks before, but at that moment, Dahlia realized Enid was lovely.

"This is Grant Adams. Those are his twin daughters you've been talking to."

"Hello," Enid said a bit shyly.

Dahlia forced herself not to stare as Grant suddenly became gregarious and talkative—a total metamorphosis. She excused herself and went to help Rod rearrange the room.

"I've never seen Grant smile so much," Rod commented.

"Nor Enid. Since her husband left, she's opted out of a lot of things in the community. She always uses Ben as an excuse." Dahlia blinked when Grant's smile widened. "I should invite them both for dinner so they can get to know each other better."

"I thought Grant was *your*…friend," Rod said.

"He is. I am. I mean, we're just friends," Dahlia told him then faltered to a stop, realizing how flustered she sounded when Rod lifted an eyebrow. "I mean, Grant needs someone in his life." The more she insisted, the more misgiving bubbled inside her.

She wasn't interested in him, so why shouldn't he look for a wife elsewhere?

Perhaps because she *was* interested in him.

Dahlia pushed the thought away and went to organize the groups for tumbling, trampoline and parallel bars. As usual, Dahlia lost herself in teaching the moves she'd adored as a child. At the end of class, she went over to talk to Enid.

"I wonder if you and Ben would like to come for dinner tomorrow night?" she asked Enid as they stored equipment.

Enid looked slightly surprised. "That's kind of you, Dahlia. We'd love to come. Can I bring anything?"

They discussed the menu for a few minutes; then Enid went to collect Ben. Dahlia walked over to Grant, who was helping the twins with their jackets.

"Would you three like to come over for dinner tomorrow night?" she asked. The twins bounced with excitement, making her smile.

"We'd love to share dinner with you. Could I contribute something?" He gave her a droll smile. "Pickles, perhaps?"

"Pickles would be great. And bring an appetite. See you then."

"Dahlia," he said before she could walk away. She stopped. "Thanks for helping me tonight. Meeting people, getting involved—it just seems to take so much extra effort for me. But you've shown me that it's worth it," he said with a smile. "I had a great time tonight."

Dahlia's heart seemed to skip a beat. "Good. And you're welcome." She struggled to ignore her response to that smile.

"We'd better go. See you tomorrow." After Glory and Grace hugged her, he ushered them out.

Dahlia watched as he gave Enid a wave.

Maybe she should have talked to Laurel before she set this plan in motion.

As she walked home alone, Dahlia planned the menu for her guests. But no matter how she tried to take her mind off Grant, she couldn't seem to do it. Grant was helping her with the go-karts, she reminded herself. Helping him find the girls a mom was the least she could do to repay him.

After all, it didn't matter if she found Grant

attractive, or kind, or anything else. She didn't want the kind of marriage he was offering.

So why did she now regret having introduced him to Enid?

Dahlia had clearly gone to a lot of work for what Grant had thought would be a simple dinner. He noticed the extra place settings.

"I hope you won't mind," Dahlia said as she hung their jackets in the closet. "I invited Kurt—a friend of mine—and Enid to join us."

"Another friend who needs a love life?" he teased.

"Kurt?" She chuckled as she shook her head. "Kurt's already happily married. His wife, Trina, is a nurse practitioner. She flies out to Arviat in Nunavut two or three times a week. Kurt hates to cook."

"So you have him over for dinner." She nodded and Grant thought, *typical Dahlia*. She gave a lot to her friends.

She asked the twins if they wanted to help her make a salad. Amid their jubilant responses, Dahlia invited Grant to have a seat and relax.

"I'd rather help you and the twins," he said. "I could cut the pickles if you like."

"You actually brought pickles?" She chuckled when he retrieved the big jar he'd set on the floor near the door. "Then you have yourself a job."

As Grant worked, he couldn't help marveling at the sense of camaraderie he felt working with Dahlia. Everything seemed fun. The twins, who'd whined earlier about leaving their dolls behind, now giggled as they chopped mushrooms with plastic knives.

"I invited Enid to join us because I noticed you two seemed to hit it off last night. Is that okay…or will it make things awkward?" she asked.

Grant looked at her. The hesitation in her voice seemed out of character.

"Sometimes it's easier to talk and get to know people in a homey situation," she added. A pink flush tinged her cheeks, adding to her beauty. Her upswept hair and a hint of makeup emphasized her hazel eyes.

In that moment, Grant was surprised to discover that he thought Dahlia was gorgeous. He was so startled, he started to backpedal immediately.

"I guess that's true, though it wasn't hard to talk to Enid," he said nonchalantly. "She seems very friendly."

"She's a lovely person. A little reserved, perhaps. She doesn't trust anyone easily."

"With her history, you can't blame her for

not being interested in starting another relationship," Grant agreed.

"She told you she's not interested?" Dahlia asked, sounding shocked.

"Yes. Actually, I think that's why it was so easy to relax with her." Dahlia gave him a look he didn't understand. He mused on it as he took the knife from Glory before she could crush the life out of an innocent tomato.

"Good job, Glory," Dahlia said. She scooped the tomatoes into the salad as the doorbell rang. "That must be the others."

Enid, Ben and a tall, lean man Dahlia introduced as Kurt joined them.

"Everything is ready," Dahlia said once she'd stored their jackets. "Why don't we sit at the table?"

She asked Kurt to say grace. His low tones vibrated with reverence as he asked a blessing on the food. Then Dahlia filled everyone's glasses with punch.

"So you're helping Dahlia with the go-karts," Kurt said to Grant. "That's great. I've been out over the track a couple of times, checking it out. I was an engineer before I retired." When Dahlia returned to the kitchen, he confided, "I'm a bit worried about that track."

"Why?" Grant kept his own voice low.

"I think it's going to take more money than

Dahlia's budgeted," Kurt murmured. "I'll explain later. Great salad," he said as Dahlia returned to the table. "Some loving hands chopped those mushrooms."

"Grace and I did that." Glory held up her hands. "Daddy, do we have loving hands?"

Grant hesitated, uncertain how to answer.

"Hands that do things for others are always loving hands," Kurt told them with a wink.

Dahlia skillfully drew Enid and Ben into the conversation and kept everyone laughing with stories about some of her customers' requests. By the time she served dessert, Grant felt totally comfortable with Kurt.

"I'm sorry to hurry away," Enid said half an hour later. "I've a lot of papers to grade. But it's been so lovely, Dahlia. Thank you."

"Thank you for bringing the squash. I'm going to need your recipe." Dahlia waved them out, smiling at Ben's sudden shyness when the twins hugged him. "Coffee?" she asked as the twins returned to a game they'd begun.

"Love to, but I can't. I've got a web consult in twenty minutes," Kurt said, rising. "I might be formally retired, but I still work the odd private engineering job. Difference is, I choose which jobs." He enveloped Dahlia in a bear hug. "Thank you, sweet one. I loved it. Trina will be relieved I didn't touch the stove."

Grant watched Kurt give the giggling twins the same bear hug he'd lavished on Dahlia.

"Call me Uncle Kurt," he ordered. "One of these days I'm going to take you fishing, if your dad agrees."

The twins squealed with delight as he set them down. Kurt held out a hand.

"Nice to meet you, Grant."

"Likewise," he said, holding Kurt's gaze. "What we were talking about earlier—I had a couple of questions. Can you do coffee tomorrow at three? I promised Dahlia I'd help her with the track at four."

"Sounds good." Kurt left.

"Well, you two sure hit it off." Dahlia said, smiling when he moved to help her clear the table.

"He's great. I'm glad you introduced us." The truth was Grant could hardly wait to hear Kurt's opinion on the track. If there were issues, he wanted Dahlia to know about them before she went any further with her project.

"Sorry my plan with Enid didn't quite work out the way I'd hoped."

"It was nice of you to try." Without thinking, Grant reached out and touched her hand before she could grasp another dish.

The green of her eyes seemed to darken to

match the emerald tone of the sheath she wore. "I'll think of someone else. Don't worry."

"Thank you."

"Don't thank me yet." She looked at him for a moment longer, then withdrew her hand when the twins called out for her to join their game.

"Go and play with them," he urged. "Let me clean this up." When she hesitated, he said, "They've been looking forward to playing with you all day."

She finally agreed. When he checked a few minutes later, Dahlia was sitting on the floor in her lovely dress, smiling from ear to ear as she played chutes and ladders, completely unaware that the twins had stuck a clown face on her back. Tiny auburn wisps framed her face in curls, one of which slipped down her cheek to rest against her slim white neck.

How lovely she was. How absolutely perfect she'd be as a mom.

As a mom—that was all he wanted from her, wasn't it?

Confused by his thoughts of his lovely hostess, Grant sighed and returned to loading the dishwasher. He had a hunch that whomever Dahlia found for him was not going to measure up to Dahlia herself.

* * *

The following day Grant shifted in the booth at Common Grounds, the local café.

"So tell me your concerns," he said, impatient to hear Kurt's opinion.

Kurt leaned back. "From what I've heard," Kurt said, "Dahlia was told that fixing old tires along the edge of the old road will suffice. It won't. The shoulders are crumbling and badly weathered. The whole thing needs to be resurfaced, but that won't happen."

"Why not?" Grant asked, his stomach dropping.

"Paving equipment and crews are in short supply here because it's so expensive to bring everything by rail. Cement is out because the cost would be astronomical to remove the old surface."

Grant's heart sank at his words.

"I don't think she can afford to do major repairs, but without doing that preliminary work, there isn't much point in doing anything else." Kurt tented his fingers. "There's got to be a way to find some money. Dahlia's project is too worthwhile to give up."

"That means fund-raising?" Grant frowned. "Is that possible?"

"Oh, yeah." Kurt nodded. "This place is big

on community. They'll come through. A prayer or two wouldn't hurt, either."

Grant raised an eyebrow.

"You don't believe in prayer?" Kurt asked.

"I haven't had much success with it," Grant admitted.

"Nobody ever said God would answer on our timetable, but if you're as concerned with Dahlia's project as you seem, it's time to ramp up your efforts." Kurt swallowed the last of his coffee, set down his cup and rose. "Because without some kind of heavenly intervention, I doubt her go-kart track is going to happen."

Grant rose, too, his head whirling. Dahlia would be devastated if she couldn't complete her project, especially since she felt she had so much to prove.

Grant said goodbye to Kurt and headed home. On the way he decided he'd look for an opportunity to tell her what he'd learned from Kurt.

"And I'll pray," he vowed. "I have to think of some way to help. It's her big dream. I don't want to see it fail."

She'd done so much for him, it seemed only fair he do what he could for her.

His heart warned that there was more to it than that, but Grant refused to stop and analyze what that might be.

He pulled up to the house, but before he could

open his front door, Lucy raced outside, her face as white as her hair.

"Why don't you answer your phone?" she asked, tears streaming down her cheeks.

"What's wrong?" Dread clamped an icy hand around his throat. He raced inside but didn't see the twins. "Where are they?"

"I don't know," she said, her voice frantic. "Grace asked for a glass of milk. I went to get it. When I came back, she and Glory were gone. Hector went to look for them."

"How long ago?" he gasped.

"Fifteen minutes?" Lucy buried her face in her hands. Then, as if regaining strength, she threw back her shoulders. "I'll stay here and pray. You go look for them. I've already alerted the police."

Guilt swelled. He wanted to blame Lucy, but it was his fault this happened. He'd failed again, having coffee when he should have been here, at home, doing his duty as a father. He'd never felt more helpless.

"My phone is on now," he said. "Call me—"

Lucy nodded and said, "Go!"

But once inside his car, Grant wasn't sure where to go. Dahlia, he decided. She'd know. He pressed the gas and headed to her store.

And prayed with every fiber of his being.

Chapter Eight

"You haven't seen them?" Staff Sergeant Dave Cramer asked Dahlia as they stood at the counter in the hardware store.

"No," she said trying to understand. "Why would Grace and Glory come here?"

"We're not sure where they went." He explained Lucy's frantic call. "I've started a search."

"Those twins are as mischievous as they come and they love to play games." Dahlia struggled to suppress her worry. "Grant must be frantic."

"I am," Grant said as he strode into the store.

"Give me a minute and I'll go with you to look for them," she promised. "Dave, this is Grant Adams, the twins' father. Grant, this is Staff Sergeant Dave Cramer. He's already looking for the twins."

"We've been trying to reach you, Mr. Adams," Dave said.

Dahlia ducked away to ask her assistant to cover for her for the rest of the day. When she returned with her jacket and truck keys, Dave was gone and Grant was pacing.

"Let's go find them," she said.

"It's my fault they took off," he growled, berating himself. She led the way to her truck.

"Let's take mine. I have four-wheel drive. We might need that. Why is it your fault, Grant?"

"I'm supposed to keep track of them." He sounded angry. "Where do we start?"

"Let's head toward your place in case they're on their way back. Who knows what those two are up to."

"I should have known Lucy couldn't handle them."

"Stop it, Grant. Blame doesn't help." Dahlia wanted to say she was to blame since she'd facilitated the twins' care with Lucy. But that wouldn't help. She pulled onto the street, glancing right and left as she drove. "Do you know what they were wearing?"

"This morning they had on those polka-dot outfits you made. It's been so warm and they wanted to show them off and…" His voice trailed away as he looked at her. "I don't know if they took jackets or not. Lucy didn't say."

Dahlia called Lucy, who reported nothing missing from the coat closet. Dahlia then called

Laurel and asked if the Lives boys could help search.

"Of course. I'll drive them in now. Keep me posted. We'll check the road on the way," she promised.

"There. We've got a lot of helpers looking," Dahlia told Grant. "Keep praying. We'll find them."

They drove in silence for several minutes toward the school. Suddenly, Grant grabbed her arm, startling her so much she slammed on the brakes.

"Sorry. I just thought of something," he explained. "Ben told the twins about a sod house the Lives boys helped build. The twins have been asking questions about it ever since."

Without another word, Dahlia wheeled the truck around and drove toward the sod house.

"Can't hurt to check it out," she said. Her heart melted at the look on Grant's face. She pressed his shoulder and let her fingers linger, trying to encourage him. She wanted to do more, to ease his burden somehow, but how?

When they arrived, they stepped out of the car and glanced around. A giggle floated to Dahlia on the breeze.

"Listen." Dahlia held her breath. It came again, faint but undeniable. Her gaze met Grant's and held.

"Be calm," she begged softly. "We don't want to terrify them. We can explain later that leaving as they did was wrong. For now let's just make sure they're safe."

His lips tightened but he nodded his agreement. Dahlia led the way. A few moments later, behind the sod house, they saw the twins crouched down in some very tall grass, playing with a black cat.

"Hello, girls," she said. "I see you've found a friend. What's his name?"

"I don't know." Glory glanced from Dahlia to her father. "Hi, Daddy. What are you doing here?"

"Daddy and I came to look for you," Dahlia said before Grant could answer. "Miss Lucy is very worried. She doesn't know where you are."

"But we left her a picture." Grace frowned. "We asked for some milk for this kitty. Miss Lucy was bringing it to us, but she took so long. This kitty started to leave so we followed it. But I drew a picture for Miss Lucy." Grace tilted her head to look at her father. "Maybe she doesn't know how to read my pictures. Do you think so, Daddy?"

"Yes, I think that's exactly right," Grant told her. "We should go home so she won't worry anymore. You don't want Miss Lucy to worry, do you?"

"Oh, no." The twins shook their heads in unison.

"What about him?" Glory said, looking at the cat. "He's hungry. He meows all the time."

"Let's bring him along, then." Dahlia reached out to pick up the cat, but it clawed at her, leaving long scratches on her arm. "Ow!"

"You have to be gentle with him, Dally." Glory frowned.

"We'll leave him here, then," Grant said. He was immediately inundated with howls of distress from the twins.

While Grant tried reasoning with his daughters, Dahlia called Dave Cramer. Then she called Lucy and finally Laurel.

"I'm sorry I dragged you and the boys out," she apologized.

"Nonsense. We all wanted to help. Since we aren't needed there, we might spend the next hour or so pulling weeds along the go-kart track." Laurel chuckled. "I take it you won't object?"

"Hardly." Dahlia was delighted that despite the emergency, they would make progress today. "I'll be there as soon as I can."

Grant motioned to Dahlia that he wanted to speak to Laurel.

"Hang on, Laurel. Grant wants to talk to you." Dahlia held out her phone. As his fingers grazed hers, a tingle zipped up her arm. When he gave her a strange look, she wondered if Grant felt it, too. "She's on the line," she managed to squeak.

"Thanks." He cleared his throat. "Laurel," he said bringing the phone to his ear. "Would you have room at Lives for a cat? I wouldn't ask, but the twins seem to have adopted one and my rental doesn't allow pets."

Dahlia could hear Laurel laughing. After a few moments, Grant handed back the phone.

"She said, 'How can it hurt to add a cat to this menagerie?'" He turned to the twins. "We can't take it home. But we can take him to Lives. They already know him there. Laurel says his name is Tux because it looks like he's wearing a tuxedo." Before they could ask, Grant explained, "A tuxedo is a black suit with a white bow tie."

"Tux. That's a good name." Grace and Glory looked at each other then nodded. "Okay, Daddy."

Dahlia could barely hide her grin at his huff of relief.

"Before we can go to Lives, we have to go home. You need to apologize to Miss Lucy for leaving without telling her. She didn't understand your picture and she was very worried." His face tightened. Dahlia knew he was trying not to show how scared he'd been. "You know the rules, girls."

"No leaving without telling." Grace nodded. "We're sorry, Daddy."

"I know you are. But you need to tell Lucy."

"Okay." Glory hefted the cat into her arms and, with Grant's help, climbed into the truck. Grace followed close behind. Grant closed the door.

"I'm sorry I took you away from work, Dahlia," he said.

"Any excuse is a good one." She smiled at him. "You did a great job with them."

"Thanks. When I was talking to Laurel, she asked me to hold a group meeting at the go-kart track site. She thinks the boys need to talk." Grant got in the truck and remained silent amid the twins' chatter until she pulled up in front of his house.

"Thank you hardly seems enough," he said after he'd lifted the twins out and sent them inside to apologize to Lucy.

"Forget it." Dahlia smiled and shook her head. "I'm just glad they're safe. If you'll wait, I'll close up the store and come back to pick you up. We could go out to the track together."

He shook his head. "You don't have to—"

"I *want* to, Grant. Otherwise, I wouldn't have offered." She looked directly at him. Couldn't he tell how far she would go to help him and his sweet daughters? Dahlia didn't realize she'd been holding her breath until he finally nodded "Give me fifteen minutes?"

"Take however long you need. And thank you." He smiled. "I keep saying that to you."

"Let's keep it that way," she teased and drove off.

By the time Dahlia changed into jeans and a work jacket, packed a couple of thermoses filled with hot chocolate, gotten back into her car and pulled up in front of his house, twenty-five minutes had passed. It took several minutes more for the girls to settle the now fractious cat.

"Are we going on a picnic?" Grace asked, eyeing the basket.

"No. But it's hard work pulling weeds. I thought we might like a drink and some cookies. Do you like hot chocolate?" When the twins didn't immediately answer, she glanced at Grant.

"I don't know if they've ever had it," he told her. "Eva felt sugar was very bad for kids and cut it from their diet as completely as she could."

"Oh, why didn't you tell me? Here I gave them dessert and—"

"Dahlia." His eyes rested on her like a soothing caress. "I've accepted that while Eva's ways were good, I can't completely adhere to them.

I think a few sips of hot chocolate and a bite of dessert are okay."

"Well, look at you," she said with a huge smile. "Here you are making fatherly decisions about your kids. I guess you have accepted that."

"Yes, I have," Grant said proudly as he returned her smile. They got in the car and drove to the track. "Oh, look," Dahlia exclaimed as they pulled up. "Teddy's here. We should be able to put up that hut in no time."

The girls bounded ahead of them, straight to Arlen, and handed him the cat. He set it down, grimacing when its claws scratched his arm. His frown vanished when the twins ordered him to bend down so they could hug him. To Dahlia's amazement, a soft look of yearning spread across Arlen's face and he gathered the girls close.

"You scared me," he said. "Why did you leave without telling anyone? That's dangerous."

For the first time since they'd found the twins, Dahlia saw chastened looks on their faces.

"We're sorry."

"Okay, but next time, don't leave before asking permission." Arlen's voice held a tightness that surprised Dahlia. "Promise?"

"We promise." The two faces remained solemn for about ten seconds before their charming smiles returned. "Can we help with Dally's go-kart track?"

"Do you mind when they call you Dally?" Grant asked.

"No," she said truthfully. But the sound of that nickname brought back so many memories. Tears welled.

"But you're crying." Grant turned her to face him.

"Happy tears," she whispered, wiping her tears with her sleeve. "That nickname brings back memories."

"Good ones, I hope." He took a tissue from his pocket and dabbed at her cheeks, his touch gentle, his gaze warm and comforting. "You must miss your grandmother and your parents a lot."

"Sometimes I do," she admitted. "I expect my parents to appear one day unannounced and insist on inspecting what I've been doing." Her shoulders went back defensively. "That's why I need to get this done. I need to show them this track in action. Maybe then they'll accept that I'm not their weak, helpless daughter anymore."

"Maybe they'll come to see *you,* because they miss you." His quiet, pensive voice soothed.

"Maybe," Dahlia agreed. But she doubted it. How could Grant understand? Grant would never betray the twins as her parents had betrayed her. He was committed to doing his best for them. All her parents had wanted was for her to marry someone who could take over their empire.

As they approached Teddy Stonechild, he thrust out his hand and introduced himself to Grant. "Those two sweet things of yours must be a handful. I heard about their adventure this afternoon. Must have been hard on you." After Grant agreed Teddy turned to Dahlia. "So what can I help with?"

She told him about the hut and, as expected, Teddy organized the boys into crews to put it together. Almost two hours later, as dusk settled over the taiga, the hut was finished.

Grant had already met most of Lives' staff; Sara, Lives' head cook, and her husband, Kyle, who was the activities director at Lives. He'd also met Rick Salinger, the local minister, and his wife, Cassie, and their son, Noah, all of whom had arrived in time for Pastor Rick to say a blessing over the structure. Dahlia bowed her head, filled with gratitude that this part had gone so easily.

"I can't thank you all enough," she said. "We're one step closer to making this dream a reality."

"It's our dream, too," Laurel assured her with

a smile. "The boys decided on that this afternoon."

A loud cheer went up, but Dahlia noticed that Arlen didn't join in.

"It's so warm I thought we could have a picnic," Laurel continued. "Sara and Kyle are bringing it. In the meantime, we'll help Rick build a fire by collecting some material we can burn in it."

Everyone began to scavenge brush. Dahlia moved closer to Grant and nudged him when Arlen squatted to show the twins what to pick up. The look he shared with her made Dahlia feel as if they were proud parents. Grant seemed comfortable with letting the twins stay with Arlen. She admired the growth he'd made as a father and savored the moment they shared together.

Sara and Kyle arrived and within minutes had set up a table and loaded it with hot-dog fixings. Dahlia added her thermoses of hot chocolate and her cookies. Then she held Sara's baby while the Lives' cook supervised.

Dahlia cuddled the small body close, savoring the scent of baby powder. She had so much love bottled up inside. If only God would touch Arlen's heart, let him accept the love she longed to give.

"Come and watch us, Dally," the twins called,

dipping their hot dogs dangerously close to the flames of the fire. Fortunately Arlen was there to look after them.

"You're very good with them, Arlen," Dahlia told him sincerely. He gave her a sideways glance.

"They're just little. You have to watch them all the time at this age. They can get into so much trouble." Then, as if he'd said too much, Arlen clamped his lips together and turned away.

A moment later, Grant approached her, his gaze moving from the baby she cuddled to her face. "You're a natural, aren't you?" Dahlia blushed. Before she could answer, he continued, "Do you have a moment? I want to talk to you. Privately."

Grant's sober face worried Dahlia. But at that moment, just as Laurel asked the boys to gather round Grant, Sara came to take her baby. Though she was curious about Grant's need to talk, there was nothing for Dahlia to do but find a spot to sit and listen.

"This track you're transforming," Grant began. "It's old. It had another use in the past. Together you're remaking it, turning something useless and abandoned into something new and worthwhile. I want to warn you that there will be hardships along the way."

She knew he was talking to the boys, but Grant stared straight at her. Dahlia felt a frisson of worry build and climb up her spine. Something was wrong. She could feel it.

Oh, Lord, her heart begged. *Whatever it is, please don't let it end my dream.*

As Grant spoke, he grew very aware of Dahlia's tension. He hated seeing her so worried.

However, he'd come up with a possible solution to the problem Kurt had pointed out.

"Think about ways you can reshape problems in your past into opportunities for your future. All it takes is some planning and determination. If you want to talk to me, I'm available for you."

Laurel asked Rick to close off the evening with prayer then asked the boys to help Teddy extinguish the fire.

"That was a very inspiring talk," Dahlia said to Grant.

"I agree," Laurel said. "I believe some of the boys are beginning to realize this is the time to plan for when they leave here."

"I hope so." His gaze rested on Arlen, who sat nearby on a log, one sleeping twin on each knee.

"I don't know if he's had a breakthrough yet. His facade seems as tough as ever, but you never know what God is working on beneath that mask." Laurel smiled at Grant and Dahlia, then hurried away to get the van packed up.

"He still pushes me away," she said to Grant.

"I think it's because he doesn't want to admit he's not totally self-reliant," Grant explained. "To have to rely on someone else is a weakness he can't yet accept." The longing on her face touched him and he had to stop himself from comforting her physically "Can you collect the twins and take them to the truck? I want to speak to Teddy for a minute."

"Sure." Dahlia looked pleased by the opportunity to interact with Arlen and the twins.

Grant moved away, watching as she approached Arlen. He wanted to remind her that Arlen would respond better to firmness. But he stemmed the urge, mentally willing the boy not to hurt her.

"Grant wants me to get the twins in the truck, Arlen," she said softly. "Would you mind helping?"

"Okay." He glanced at the redheads nestled against either shoulder, eased their sleeping bodies a bit, then rose. "I can carry them."

"Are you sure?" When he nodded, Dahlia led the way to the truck.

Grant couldn't hear the rest of their conversation, but when the interior truck light came on, he saw yearning on her face. He also saw a softening in Arlen's hard eyes as he eased Glory onto the seat, leaving Dahlia to belt her in while he tenderly carried Grace to the other side. After fastening her seat belt, Arlen brushed his knuckles against her pink-flushed cheek then carefully closed the door.

Dahlia moved beside him. She said something and Arlen's mask slid back in place. He nodded, jerked away from the hand she'd placed on his shoulder and quickly strode to Laurel's van, a lonely figure in the faint light of the remaining coals. Dahlia gazed after his retreating figure, tears on her cheeks.

Laurel had said Teddy was deeply involved with Lives. Maybe he could help make Dahlia's dream come true. Grant arranged a meeting with Teddy.

Then back at Grant's place, Dahlia helped him put the twins to bed.

Grant gazed at their sleeping faces, reliving the terror that had filled him when they'd gone missing. It couldn't happen again. They needed him. He adored them as he'd never imagined he could. He could not lose them.

When he returned to the living room, Dahlia confronted him. "What did you want to talk to me about?"

Grant didn't soften what Kurt had told him.

It was better she know the whole truth up front. He laid it out as plainly as he'd been told.

"If it's hopeless, why did you let us put up that hut tonight?" Her face showed the strain she usually hid. "If the track isn't going to happen—"

"Because I think it *can* happen," he emphasized.

"Grant, I don't have any more money. I'm already scraping the budget to get this track functional." She flopped into his armchair.

"So we'll fund-raise," he told her. "We'll plan some events to raise what you need to complete the project."

A rush of joy filled Grant when the stress lines around her eyes eased. Finally, this was something he could do for Dahlia.

"Thank you. You have no idea how much this means to me, Grant."

"Yes, I do," he said softly. Dahlia had never looked lovelier than she did now with her mussed hair, her face almost devoid of makeup. Grant was surprised by how much he wanted to kiss her.

"I promised I'd do my best and I intend to," he said, try to rid himself of the image of Dahlia in his arms.

Don't let me fail her.

Dahlia's green eyes locked on his then shifted. Surely she hadn't read his thoughts? But why did she seem so nervous.

"*I* promised to help you find a mom for the twins," Dahlia said, speaking quickly. Her smile didn't reach her eyes. "Come to the store tomorrow at five and I'll introduce you to Carolina."

Did he want to meet Carolina? And even if he did, how could she compare to Dahlia? Bemused by his thoughts, Grant followed her to the door.

"Thanks a lot for helping tonight." Her hazel eyes barely met his.

"Thanks for helping me look for the twins today. You're a good friend."

At the word *friend,* an odd expression flickered across her face. Then she said good-night and climbed into her truck. Grant watched her taillights disappear.

She *was* a good friend, but Dahlia Wheatley felt like a lot more than just a friend to Grant.

However, Grant couldn't afford to consider more than a business partnership with any woman, especially Dahlia. Sooner or later he'd fail her, and hurt her. His past was a guarantee of that.

And Dahlia was too special to be hurt by his inadequacies.

It was better if he end his wayward thoughts about her. They could only be friends. No matter how lovely she was.

Chapter Nine

"So let's review what we've got for the fundraiser so far." A week later, Grant stood before the men he'd met at Lives, who he'd come to consider friends. "Kyle, you have a turkey shoot planned?"

"Adults and kids," Kyle confirmed. "Preceded by a barbecue chicken dinner supplied by Polar Bear Pizza. Half the tickets are already sold."

"Great. Now, Teddy. Your idea?" Grant was thrilled about how quickly people had come together to help Dahlia.

It certainly said a lot about how Churchill felt about her. Not that he was surprised.

"Free accommodation for six people over Christmas and New Year's at my hotel in Vancouver," Teddy said.

"That's very generous."

And on and on it went. Projects organized by

men who saw opportunity in Dahlia's project. Humbled that they'd chosen him, the newcomer, as their leader, Grant thanked them.

"Dahlia's done a lot for Churchill. It's about time we gave back to her." Kurt shared a grin with the other men. "I've arranged for the shoulders of that road to be built up. My company will cover materials, but we need contractors and equipment."

"I know a couple of guys who could do the work," someone volunteered. "But we'd have to pay for the equipment."

"Maybe we could rent the town's." Rick spoke from the back of the room. "The church's benevolent fund could cover that."

"So the road work can begin right away with Kurt in charge." Grant waited for his nod. "Any other ideas?"

A man Grant didn't know rose.

"Jack Campbell. My wife, Alicia, and I will sponsor a Thanksgiving Day dinner at Northern Lights Lodge. We'll ask for donations to the go-kart track."

"Great idea. Not having to cook a big meal on that day is probably a dream for lots of ladies," Grant enthused.

"I always said this is a community beyond all others," Dahlia spoke from the back of the room, startling many who hadn't realized she'd arrived. "You've all proven me right. Thank you so much."

"The question is, will all this raise enough money?" Teddy asked.

All eyes turned to Grant.

"There's no way to know that yet," he said. "But if we can't raise enough money to complete the track before freeze-up, we'll put everything on hold and continue to fund-raise through the winter."

"Oh, but—" Dahlia bit her lip, her disappointment obvious.

"The boys would have lots of time to get those karts you found operational—that is, if we could find a garage or shed where they could work, and a teacher," Grant said, hoping someone would have a solution.

"And if we can get them here," Kyle added.

"Anything else we need to discuss?" When no one responded, Grant rose. "Let's meet in a week to discuss our progress."

The group broke up. Grant looked for Dahlia but couldn't find her, so he hurried out of the town hall. He had less than fifteen minutes left in his lunch hour before starting his class at the high school and he hadn't yet eaten the peanut-butter sandwich he'd packed this morning. Then, his car door opened and Dahlia slid inside.

"I just wanted to say thanks again," she said.

"And to bring you this." The unmistakable aroma of fried onions on a hamburger made his stomach rumble. "I figured you wouldn't have much time for lunch but I thought we could eat together. Okay?"

"Very okay," he agreed as he unwrapped the foil bundle. He opened it, took a bite and closed his eyes. "This tastes so good."

She grinned, took a bite of her own and then blinked. "I forgot," she mumbled and reached into her bag to produce two bottles of lemonade. "I brought these, too."

"Perfect." Grant savored the tang of his lemonade as it slid down his parched throat.

"I'm surprised you'll eat with me after my matchmaking failures. I truly had no idea that introducing you to Carolina would bring so many questions. Believe me, I didn't know she was going through a third divorce. She never talks about her personal life."

"She was just being cautious," Grant said, suddenly not quite as hungry as he'd been. "But Ida—now that lady scared the daylights out of me."

"Me, too." Dahlia shuddered. "I was also very embarrassed."

"Why?" Grant grinned at the way Dahlia ducked her head and hid her eyes beneath her lashes. Her cheeks were hot pink.

"Ida seems like such a sweet, quiet woman. She adores her Sunday school kindergarten group so I thought she'd make a good candidate. But when I heard her pumping the twins for information about you, I could hardly believe it."

"Given her shock at the twins' answers, I guess I'm not the kind of father she expected." Grant burst out laughing.

"I'm sorry about asking you to meet those two ladies," she apologized again. "I know I promised I'd help you find someone, but—"

"Maybe we should give the whole matchmaking thing a rest for a while," he interrupted.

Dahlia's eyes darkened to emerald. The confusion he saw in them grabbed at his heart.

"I still want to find a mom for the girls." He struggled to find the right words. "But we both have so much on our plates right now. I want to help the Lives boys as much as I want to see your project succeed."

"And?" Dahlia waited.

"I have to work with the school students as well as ensure the twins properly settle into their lives here," Grant said. "Maybe this isn't the right time to be thinking about changing yet another part of their lives."

"And you said you didn't know anything about being a father." A faint smile tugged at Dahlia's lips. "Yet you make these responsible, well-thought-out decisions about your girls' welfare. Hate to tell you, Grant, but that *is* fatherhood."

"Those aren't the important decisions," he protested.

"Aren't they?" She gathered up their trash, then caught his gaze. "I don't believe there are any unimportant decisions when it comes to children. God blessed you with the twins. I'm pretty sure He knew what He was doing." She pushed open the door and stepped out of his car. "I'll see you later at Lives."

"Thanks for lunch," he said, marveling at the way Dahlia could cut right to the heart of the matter. "Will you be there by five o'clock?"

"Provided I can get away. I hope we finish with the last of those weeds today so Kurt can start on the road edges. Bring the twins."

"I'm not sure about that. Aren't the polar bears around right now?" Worry pricked at him. "I don't want to endanger them."

Dahlia shook her head as she chuckled. "Arlen's appointed himself the girls' personal protector. A bear wouldn't get within ten feet of the twins." With a wave she was gone.

Grant drove to the school.

Dahlia is so sure about You. Why is it I never feel sure of anything? Is it because I'm not as close to You as I should be?

The prayer slipped out without thought, surprising Grant with how good it felt to confide in God again. He decided to get up half an hour earlier in the morning so he could return to reading his Bible before the day started, a habit he'd learned from Eva.

Maybe then God would help him gain assurance about his decisions.

Though Grant wondered if he'd ever reach Dahlia's level of certainty about God, past thoughts that had once reminded him that when he'd needed God as a child, God hadn't been there, were now coming less frequently.

Maybe if he kept trying, one day he'd get as comfortable with God as Dahlia.

Grant decided there was a lot he could learn from her. She never ceased to amaze him.

As Dahlia tugged at the remaining weeds along the old road, she hummed a little chorus from church. Every so often she glanced over her shoulder just to be sure no furry white polar bear crept up on her—and then mocked the silly fears Grant had raised. The bears hadn't yet returned to Churchill or a notice would have gone out. The unseasonably warm days seemed to have slowed everything, including their arrival. Anyway, the fence protected her.

After a while, she forgot about everything

but the beauty of the day as she silently worshipped God.

"You're making great progress." She jumped and turned to find Grant studying her, a smile threading through his voice. "It doesn't look like you need me," he said with a grin.

"I'll take all the help I can get. Feel free to grab a weed. There's no shortage." Her eyes widened when she noticed the girls trailing behind him, their faces sad. "What's up with those two? They're usually bouncing."

"They thought Arlen would be here," Grant explained. "They're crazy about him. I promised them that if they behaved they could come and see him. If he doesn't show, I'm in deep trouble."

"And here I thought I was their favorite person." Dahlia faked a frown. "Oh, well, as long as they pull weeds, I won't be offended."

"They might pull the tops off," he said. "But that's the most you should expect."

Dahlia couldn't stop the laughter that spilled out. Grant was such fun to be with. She couldn't remember feeling so comfortable with another person in a long time. His sense of humor matched hers, and she loved to make him laugh. She refused to think about the days after the project was complete when she wouldn't see him nearly as often.

"Here comes our help," she said as the Lives boys arrived.

Dahlia watched as Arlen joyfully embraced the twins, then showed them how to remove a few tiny weeds with the miniature spades he produced.

"I'm sorry, Dahlia. I imagine it must hurt to have him snub you."

"It does hurt. But I'm trying to leave it with God and let Him sort out the ways and means."

"It's as easy as that?" Grant took the huge weed she'd pulled, added his own to the pile in the middle of the road.

"Easy?" Dahlia took out her frustration on another weed. "It's not easy at all," she huffed as the roots came free. "But trusting God means believing He will handle things for my best interest. If I worry, I'm second-guessing Him and that's not trust."

"I second-guess God all the time," Grant admitted, continuing to work beside her.

"It's an easy habit to fall into. We tend to fall back on the easiest route. If we'd only trust, we'd realize that's far easier than worrying."

"I'm beginning to realize that."

As Grant worked silently beside her, she realized that he was changing, gradually building the faith he'd once claimed he'd given up on. She prayed for him silently as they worked side by side for the next half hour. They paused only for occasional checks on the twins, who were enjoying their time with Arlen.

When the sun set and it grew too dim to work, Laurel coaxed everyone back to Lives, where they gathered around the big kitchen table to eat Sara's stew.

The boys joked about the go-kart track until Rod asked Laurel, "Is the track a sure thing? Or is there a chance we're doing all this work for nothing?" He frowned. "I've heard rumors."

"Grant and Dahlia are the project leaders," Laurel said. "Let's hear what they have to say."

"When I first began this project, I projected costs with the information I had." Dahlia met each boy's gaze directly. "At that point I had enough funds to complete the project. Since then I've been told more work is needed. Grant is spearheading a community group that is raising funds to meet expenses. Grant?"

Dahlia listened with burgeoning pride as he explained the fundraisers.

"You guys could help by making posters for advertising for the various events," he suggested. "If you could spare a few minutes to help out, we'd appreciate it. But you have to clear everything with Laurel first."

"What about the machines?" Arlen demanded from his place between Grace and Glory.

"What's the point of doing all this work on the track if we haven't got anything to run on it?"

"There are used machines sitting in Thompson until we have funds to transport them here." Dahlia focused on Arlen. "We'll need a place to repair them. Perhaps you could ask around."

"Me?" He glared at her. "This is your project."

"No, it's a project designed to benefit those who come to Lives." With all eyes focused on her, Dahlia's cheeks warmed, but she refused to back down from Arlen's unspoken challenge. "It will take participation on your part to make it happen."

"I might not be here by the time it's working." He glared. "Why should I help?"

"Why wouldn't you?" Grant challenged. "Why should Dahlia stick her neck out to do this for *you?*"

Dahlia could see the boys were listening. *Keep going,* she mentally begged Grant.

"Let's think about this some more," he said. "What is the point of giving to others? Isn't it easier to grab for yourselves and let the other guy fend for himself?"

"Easier, maybe," Rod agreed. "But aren't people stronger when they work as a group?"

"Why?" Grant leaned back and waited.

"Because groups are always more powerful

than a single person," Rod said. "That's why I got into a gang." The other boys laughed, but they knew what he meant.

Dahlia listened, fascinated by Grant's methods. He said little, yet he skillfully drew out each boy and then led them to the discovery that giving to others could make their own lives better.

"So," he said, drawing the discussion to a close. "We've got Dahlia getting this go-kart track up and running. A bunch of people in town are working to make it happen. I'm trying to help, though some might say I'm more a hindrance," he joked. "And you guys voted to go with this project. So besides pulling weeds, what will you contribute?"

Silence fell around the room as the boys risked a glance at their neighbor and then down.

"Maybe next time we talk, you'll have ideas of how you can play a bigger part in this project," he said. "Now I think I'd better take my girls home before Arlen's arms go to sleep holding them."

Laughter ended the session. It was the perfect note to finish on. Once they'd left Lives and tucked the girls into Grant's vehicle, Dahlia told him so.

"I don't know how you always hit the right note," she murmured. "But God has certainly gifted you. Those boys got the message loud and clear without you preaching at them."

"That's the best way." Grant smiled. "I'd better go. Morning comes earlier all the time."

"Want to bring the girls over tomorrow night? I'm making cookies for Thanksgiving."

"But that's a week away," Grant said in surprise.

"I'm making *a lot* of cookies," she said.

"I can certainly help eat them." He waggled his eyebrows, and Dahlia couldn't help but laugh.

"In exchange for your inexpert help, I'll throw in dinner. Six-thirty?"

He nodded and climbed in his car.

"Good night, girls," Dahlia said, sticking her head in Grant's window. The sleepy girls blew her kisses.

As she drew away, her face came within an inch of Grant's. Their gazes locked. Dahlia couldn't breathe. The slightest movement forward and they'd be kissing....

No!

Dahlia couldn't get sidetracked; couldn't weaken and let her heart get involved. A relationship meant being vulnerable to hurt and betrayal, and she didn't want to go through that again.

"Good night, Grant," she murmured and stepped back.

But as she pulled away, she felt something inside her cry out.

Why did being strong have to hurt so much?

"I can't believe you are actually encouraging them to make a mess." Grant felt his fingertips curl at the flour Glory had just dumped all over the counter.

"We can always clean up messes," Dahlia said as she scooped up the white powder. "The important thing about making cookies is to enjoy the process. Here." She handed him a cookie cutter in the shape of a turkey, then pointed to the slab of dough she'd rolled out. "Daddy should cut the first cookie, right?"

"Right." The twins grinned up at him, waiting.

"How do I do it?" Grant wished he'd made some excuse to leave the girls with Dahlia. Showing his utter ineptitude at making cookies was bad enough, but sooner or later, Dahlia would figure out he hated messes. And then she'd dig to find out why.

He did *not* want to go into that. Ever.

"Pick a spot and push the cutter into it." She smiled at him. "Easy."

Easy for her to say. He plunged it into the center of the dough, then quickly yanked it back out. Half of the dough stuck to his cutter. The rest remained on the counter.

Again his body tensed at the mess he'd created.

"You need more flour so it doesn't stick." Dahlia's hand closed over his, guided it to the flour container and carefully dipped it in. "Try again."

Stunned by how much he wanted her hand to remain on his, Grant froze.

Was he beginning to care for Dahlia?

Of course he cared about her. She was a good friend. She helped him meet people, helped with the twins. Of course he cared *about* her.

But care *for* her?

"What's wrong?" Dahlia's hazel eyes seemed to gaze right into his mind. The twins were staring, too.

"Where I should place it? There must be a method." He strove for a normal tone.

"In cookie-making, you find your own method." Dahlia's gaze remained on him. He knew she wasn't fooled by his offhand tone.

He shoved the cutter into the corner of the dough.

"Lift it slowly, Daddy." Now Grace placed her tiny hand on his. "So it doesn't break."

Grant drew the cutter slowly upward, revealing a perfect turkey.

"You did it, Daddy!" Glory cheered as if he'd just completed a marathon.

"It's an excellent turkey." Dahlia moved his work to a cookie sheet. "Now do some more. Try to get them a little closer together."

She nudged his hand slightly to the left. Again the spike of electricity flared.

"You're doing great." She smiled at him, then turned to the twins. "Your dad's ahead. Get cutting, you two."

Grace and Glory were experts compared to Grant. Wheat sheaves, scarecrows and horns of plenty multiplied beneath their small hands. There seemed no end to the dough.

"What are all of these for?" he asked.

"Every year I do a cookie-decorating afternoon at the nursing home," Dahlia explained.

"Surely a small place like Churchill doesn't have this many residents." Grant couldn't imagine how a few seniors would eat so many cookies.

"No," she conceded, a smile tugging the corners of her lovely mouth. "But we eat some, we break some, we give some to shut-ins and we use the rest at our Thanksgiving tea."

"Aren't *we* going to decorate any?" Glory asked, her face falling.

"Of course. But not tonight. Tonight is for making them and you're not finished yet."

Dahlia rolled out yet another slab of dough. This time she handed him a pumpkin-shaped cutter. "You can do a few of these now that you're an expert," she teased with a wink.

This was the most family-oriented thing he and the girls had done since Eva had died. The mess still bothered Grant, but he'd begun to see Dahlia's method. She didn't obsess about a dusting of flour on the floor, bits of dough clinging to cupboard handles or the stack of dirty dishes in the sink because she knew she'd clean up when they were finished.

The twins beamed with happiness. That was worth a lot more than his inner angst over the memories of his father's obsessive-compulsive behavior.

"Did you make Thanksgiving cookies when you were a child, Dahlia?" he asked.

"With my grandmother." Dahlia pulled a pan of golden-edged cookies from the oven and slid them onto a rack. "She loved Thanksgiving. She celebrated God's generosity by making gift baskets brimming with homemade cookies. She'd deliver them along with a handmade card."

"To whom?"

Dahlia didn't immediately answer. Instead she helped the twins cut the rest of the dough, then lifted them off their stools and sent them to the bathroom to wash up. Then she answered.

"Granny Bev said she felt that God led her to those who should get her baskets." She lifted her head to meet his gaze. "I went with her every year to deliver them."

"The more I learn of your grandmother, the more amazing she sounds." Grant wished he could offer the twins the rich heritage of a loving, extended family.

"Granny Bev had a heart for God. Everything in her life centered on Him. I want to be just like her—strong, focused, making a difference."

Didn't she know? Didn't she realize?

"You already are," Grant assured her.

"Not really. She was a woman of unbending faith. I'm not." She turned away, but Grant put a hand on her arm, forcing himself not to apologize for the flour mark he left there.

"Dahlia," he murmured. "You do so much for the community, not the least of which is the go-kart project. I've also heard about how you always give a discount to those who can't afford to pay full price and how you spend hours on customers' problems, even directing them elsewhere if you think they'll get a better deal. Your grandmother would be proud."

"Thanks." Her smile didn't reach her eyes. "But those are small things, nothing that would impress my parents."

"Why does that matter so much?" Grant

asked then wondered if he should have when her face tightened.

"Because they don't see me as part of themselves, as part of the powerful, accomplished family they're so proud of." She stared at the floor. "I need to prove I'm not the weakest link."

"But you know you're not." Grant could see she didn't believe it. "Dahlia—"

"All that's left to do now is bake these." She smoothed a rubber blade over the counter, pushing the leftovers into a bowl. She placed the cutters and utensils, along with the mixing bowl, in the dishwasher and handed him a damp cloth. "Mind wiping the counters?"

He sensed that she'd deliberately cut him off because she didn't like to show her vulnerability. If there was one thing Grant could understand it was that, so he didn't press her. He simply began scrubbing, his brain slipping back to his childhood.

"Grant?" Dahlia lifted the cloth from his hands. "I think it's clean now," she said in a gentle voice.

"Yes." He shook off the past. "The girls are nodding off. I think we should go. Thank you for this. We've had a wonderful time."

She didn't ask him to stay, solidifying his theory that she wanted to be alone. She helped him dress the twins in their outerwear then handed him a paper bag, insisting they take some of the cookies home. Grant suppressed his reaction to the brush of her fingers against his and shepherded the twins out the door.

"Thank you for everything," he said, staring into Dahlia's lovely face.

"Good night, Dally," Grace and Glory called until he closed the car door on their voices.

The twins fell silent on the drive home, as if they understood without being told that he couldn't talk to them right now, that he needed time to come to grips with Dahlia shutting him out so thoroughly. He did, but he also needed time to quash those hurtful memories he'd replayed in her kitchen.

When the girls were finally tucked in bed and the house was silent, Grant stood at the window staring into the dark night.

Memories of cleaning and polishing the cracked and tired yellow countertop in the kitchen of his childhood flooded back.

Do it again, boy. I'm not having my food prepared on this mess. Do it again with this!

Splash. He could feel the sting of the bleach on his reddened hands.

How could You possibly expect me to raise those two innocents? What if I'm like him?

For a moment, the awful horror of that possibility stuck and he couldn't break free. Then

Dahlia's face with her shining hair, pure, clear eyes and genuine smile filled his mind.

"I could share the twins with her," a tiny voice in his head whispered. "We could raise them together."

As quickly as the thought came, he dismissed it. Wasn't it obvious after tonight that Dahlia didn't see him that way? Anyway, how could he be the man Dahlia deserved?

What if he hurt her? What if he only added to the pain she already carried?

Grant could never allow that. So he'd get on with his life and keep her as a friend, a very good friend whom he cared *about*. But that was all.

He *was* going to make her go-kart dream a reality, even though he had a hunch that neither completing the track nor winning Arlen's affection would erase the hurt she'd buried inside.

Grant blinked, surprised by how very much he wanted to give Dahlia everything she wanted.

Chapter Ten

"It's not going to happen," Arlen sneered. "So why are we killing ourselves to make this track useable?"

Dahlia had just explained that before they could resurface the track, they needed to fill the cracks. Rod and Arlen were doing that as she and Grant followed with the tar topcoat.

"Do you ever stop being a naysayer?" Rod's face was red from the exertion on this unusually warm day. "Let's just get on with it."

"Who made you the boss?" Arlen yelled.

"Guys, come on. Let's cut the fighting and work together so we can get this done. Okay?"

Dahlia was relieved Grant had intervened because she was running out of ways to reach Arlen.

"Where are the twins?" After Grant poured some of the tar on the surface, she spread it across the road. They worked well together. Like partners.

"Laurel took Glory and Grace to the beach." He waited until she'd finished one section before he started another. "They're choosing pebbles for a project. Laurel said it might be the last chance before winter blows in."

"We've been lucky with the weather." For the past three days Dahlia regretted ending their cookie-making session so abruptly. She'd done it because his presence in her home with the twins had engendered dreams she couldn't afford. She needed to stop dreaming and focus on her goal. The track.

Dahlia now sensed that something had changed between them, that he'd somehow withdrawn. There was nothing she could put her finger on. He was just—different toward her.

"The twins' birthday is Saturday," Grant murmured when Arlen and Rod had moved out of range.

"They'll be six?" A bump of envy grew in Dahlia's heart. How lucky he was to share this milestone with the precocious twins. Her first instinct was to offer to help so she could be involved in the celebration, but she wasn't sure that was a good idea given this distance she felt yawning between them. "I'll bet they're excited."

"That's the problem. They want to invite their entire class to a birthday party." Panic filled his gray eyes. "I can't handle that many kids."

Dahlia felt certain it wasn't only the number of kids he was worried about. Something else ate at him.

Stick to your decision to give him space, she reminded herself. She hoped doing so would help her quell these longings to be closer to him.

Dahlia jerked upright. Was that why she was helping Grant—to get closer to him?

"Would you be available to help?" His hesitation was painfully obvious.

She wanted to say yes immediately, but she reined herself in. "With what, exactly?"

"With whatever it is one does at a child's sixth birthday."

"You've never had a birthday party?" she teased, trying to make him laugh.

"No."

At first she thought he was joking. But his eyes remained blank.

"My father wasn't into parties," Grant said, his voice giving nothing away. "And he didn't allow me to attend them either. Eva handled the twins' parties, so I truly have no clue how to make the day special, apart from buying birthday cakes and supervising some games." For a moment, his eyes lit up. "I was hoping you'd tell me how your Granny Bev would celebrate."

Even though Dahlia wanted nothing more than to help Grant, she knew doing so would put her heart at risk.

However, he was out here sweating to help with *her* project. And how could she say no to a man who understood how deeply she valued her grandmother?

"Birthday parties aren't that hard," she said. "Especially for little girls. Wearing on adults, maybe. But not difficult."

"I'd be very grateful for any advice you can offer." His gaze held hers. "I hate to keep asking you for help."

"Don't be silly." She repressed a flicker of guilt. "It will be fun. But I said I'd be at Kyle's turkey shoot that night."

"I'm going, too. The party will be over by then." Grant frowned. "I really need to find the twins a sitter. I don't like to ask Lucy for even more of her time. I'm surprised she agreed to stay on as the twins' after-school sitter after they ran away. She tried to quit but I told her that could have happened to anyone."

"Why not ask him?" Dalia inclined her head toward Arlen. "I think he'd be great at it."

"Interesting idea." Grant emptied the last of the pail on the road. "Want to switch jobs with me?"

"I thought you'd never ask," Dahlia said, half laughing, half groaning as she rubbed her back. "I didn't realize this stuff would be quite so stiff to spread."

"Just be glad it's still warm. If the sun wasn't heating things up, it wouldn't spread at all." Grant handed her the pail, then adroitly used the spreader she'd struggled to wield.

By the time she and Grant reached Rod and Arlen, the two were sitting on upturned buckets, discussing football. Apparently their argument was over.

"You guys did a great job," she praised. "I'm so glad we could finish before it turns cold."

"I'm beginning to wonder if it ever gets cold here," Arlen scoffed. "Maybe all your talk of frigid weather is fantasy."

"You wish." Dahlia laughed. "The fantasy part is believing winter won't come. It will. This is the mildest fall I've known since I arrived and I won't object if God keeps the flurries back a little while."

"You really think God cares about stuff like that?" Arlen said.

"I *know* He cares about us." Dahlia winced at the pain clouding his eyes. "We're His children. Every dad wants to give his kid their heart's desires."

"My heart's desire is to not be here," Arlen snapped.

"Where would you rather be?"

Grant started talking to Rod, leading him away so she and Arlen could be alone.

"With my sisters." He looked straight at her and for the first time there was no enmity in his gaze, just a boatload of hurt. "But that isn't going to happen."

"You won't be here forever. You'll see them soon." She reached out to touch his arm, but he jerked out of reach. "If you need to talk to someone, I'm available. So is Grant. Please don't feel you're all alone."

"But I am. My sisters are dead and my mother doesn't ever want to see me again." His eyes bored into her. "I don't think you can fix that."

"No, I'm sorry. I can't," she whispered, aghast at the burden he carried.

Arlen turned and walked away. Tears rose to clog her throat as she finally accepted that reaching Arlen was impossible.

Grant must have read something in her expression because he broke off his discussion and walked toward her.

"Can I help?" he murmured.

"I have to go home."

Desolate, she was barely aware of what was happening as Grant took over. He took her keys and helped her into her seat. He dropped the boys at Lives, drove her home and put on the kettle without asking. When the tea was ready, he set a cup in her hands. Then he squatted in front of her, placing his hands atop hers.

"What's wrong, Dahlia?"

She looked into his eyes and gave voice to her painful acceptance of the truth she had to accept.

"I don't think God's going to answer my prayer for Arlen, Grant."

Dahlia's words knifed straight into Grant's heart. He could see defeat creeping in, taking over the woman who didn't do defeat. He couldn't stand it.

"You can't know that," he reminded her. "God could be working on him without you even realizing it."

"Do you think so?"

Dahlia's earnest, desperate question sent Grant off balance. He wasn't any more certain of God's intent for her life than he was of God's intent for his own. But surely God wouldn't disappoint a woman like Dahlia, who trusted Him so completely?

"I think you have to take your own advice. Trust," he said, recalling a past conversation they'd shared. "No second-guessing, remember?"

After a moment, her head lifted, her shoulders went back and she smiled. "Maybe you're right." She slipped one hand free to cover his and squeezed. "Maybe now isn't the time to lose faith. I have to keep trusting."

Grant couldn't help it. Her sweet smile, the blaze in her hazel eyes, the trusting way she looked at him—he leaned forward and pressed his lips to hers.

At first she startled, but then Dahlia leaned into the kiss. Her hand left his to slide around his neck, drawing him closer.

For Grant these moments were poignantly special. Possibilities loomed. Perhaps he *could* love someone, Grant thought. Perhaps he wouldn't follow in his father's footsteps.

But he *was* like his dad. Eva had thought he wasn't, but she'd never known the bursts of anger that surged inside him, or his struggle to control them.

But Dahlia would know.

"I'm sorry. I shouldn't have done that." Gently, he eased away from her, anxious to put some distance between them.

"Why not?" Her hazel eyes brimmed with confusion.

"I can't get involved, Dahlia." He ignored his heart's yearning.

"But you're looking for a wife."

"I'm looking for a mother for the twins," he corrected gently. "I'm not…available for anything else."

She fell silent, her eyes searching his. Grant kept his expression as neutral as he could. Dahlia was good and sweet and lovely. It would be so easy to love her but he clung to his resolve.

"You're right," she whispered. "I can't afford to get sidetracked." She moved away from him. "We should talk about the twins' party."

Grant rose and sat opposite her. "You don't have to help, Dahlia."

"I want to, Grant. Truly."

She began listing things they could do for the girls. Grant scribbled notes, trying to forget what had just happened between them.

"Does that help?" She arched one eyebrow.

"Yes. Thanks." He checked his watch and rose. "I'd better get to work. Laurel will be bringing the girls back soon." If Dahlia realized he was eager to escape, she didn't show it.

"Thanks for helping with the track." She didn't look at him.

"That was fun. And at least Arlen revealed a little more about himself. That's progress." He waited. When she stood without looking at him, he wished he'd handled things differently. He hated the awkwardness that now loomed between them.

"Yes, it is." She walked him to the door. "I've got a big sale on Saturday at the store, but I should be able to sneak away if you need help with the party."

"No," he said in sudden decision. "You've done more than enough."

She did look at him then, surprise in her green eyes. "You're sure?"

"It's about time I do my job as a parent, don't you think?"

"You'll do fine, Grant," she said. "You love them. That's all they need."

He said good-night and left. But inside his head, a voice kept asking, *Is love really enough for the twins?*

In his heart he knew it was the only thing Dahlia wanted and he couldn't give it.

But oh, how wonderful to finally hold her in his arm, to kiss her as he'd longed to for so long. He drove home reliving every moment.

She shouldn't have done it.

But Dahlia could no more have stopped herself from peeking in on Glory and Grace's birthday party than fly to the moon.

Plus, she wanted to see Grant again.

She pulled into his driveway, trying to ignore the memory of his kiss. It was nothing, she kept telling herself, but unfortunately, her heart wasn't getting the message.

She couldn't waste time wishing otherwise. She glanced at her purse. Every nerve in her body tensed at what lay inside. A note she'd received yesterday, from her mother.

We want to see what you've accomplished up there, she'd written.

A thousand emotions raced through her. Seeing them again—would they finally accept that she was strong, capable even though the track wasn't yet finished? Had they forgiven her for leaving? Would they try to persuade her to return home?

Is she wanted their approval, Dahlia knew she had to get the track finished. She sighed, shut off her worries and walked to the house.

"Hi, Dally," the twins squealed when they opened the door.

"Happy birthday to both of you," she said, relishing their embraces. She handed each girl a gift bag.

"Thank you. We're going to open them later," Glory told her. "Right now we're having a party. Daddy made it."

"We have balloons and everything." Grace's

blue eyes shone with excitement. "And Arlen's going to take us on a treasure hunt."

"Aren't you lucky." Dahlia held her smile when Grant appeared. He looked less frazzled than she'd expected. "How's it going?"

Arlen appeared. Before he ushered the twins back to their guests, he gave Dahlia a nod. She was astonished.

"It's going better than I thought it would." Grant grinned at her surprise. "I decided to do everything I always wanted and never had. A bit crazy maybe, but it seems to be working. Arlen's been great." Grant led her to the living room.

The room was party central. The pushed-back furniture allowed plenty of room for activities. Balloons covered the ceiling. One wall featured multicolored donkey tails, though the rest of the animal had disappeared. Through the patio door, she saw tiny boats floating in a paddling pool.

Grant grasped her arm, motioning to the circle of girls sitting on the floor, with Arlen between the twins.

"They're playing a whispering game. Come into the kitchen. I've got the coffeepot on."

"It's all fantastic, Grant. I don't know why you thought you needed help."

He motioned for her to sit at the table, which was covered with cupcakes.

"Those are for decorating later." He handed her a steaming cup of coffee and sat opposite her, his face beaming.

"I always thought you were a wonderful father, Grant," she told him, surprised by the tears filling her eyes. "The twins couldn't be blessed with anyone better. You're amazing."

His eyes widened in surprise. "Thanks, Dahlia. That means a lot to me, coming from you.

She tried to gain control of her emotions, for his sake as much as hers. "How did you persuade Arlen to help?"

"He volunteered," Grant told her. "He showed up here this morning and took the twins on what he called a 'birthday walk' so I could get things ready. When I mentioned my idea of a treasure hunt, he said he knew exactly how to do it. I think being with the twins has been therapeutic for him."

"I'm sure." Dahlia wished she'd had some way to help Arlen. She was glad he'd found comfort with the twins but she knew he needed more. "Can I ask a favor? If you get a moment, can you sound out Arlen? When he told me about his sisters, I got the feeling that he's never really come to terms with their deaths."

"I've been thinking the same," Grant told her. "I've been waiting for the right opportunity to bring up the topic."

"Thank you," she said, a rush of relief filling her. Too bad she couldn't turn to Grant for answers about her parents. "So how can I help?"

"You can't. You're an invited guest," he insisted. "I didn't expect you until later. How's your sale going?"

"My staff have things well in control. I'm not needed." A burst of giggles echoed from the next room. She rose. "So what's next?"

"The treasure hunt. That's Arlen's idea," Grant told her as they walked into the living room. "I'm sure he wouldn't mind if we tag along. I want to take some pictures."

Dahlia watched as Grant snapped candid shots of the twins and their friends searching for treasure. The big surprise, however, came when Arlen mentioned how much his sisters had loved treasure hunts.

"Once I even put foil chocolate coins in a box and buried it in the backyard," he murmured, watching the kids search for the last clue. "They loved it."

"Grace and Glory love you." Dahlia smiled at him. "It's kind of you to help Grant."

"He's a good dad." Arlen watched Grant

climb a rock to get a better angle. "He doesn't think he is, though."

Curious to hear Arlen's viewpoint, she frowned. "Why do you say that?"

"Because he hesitates before he makes decisions just like my dad used to. He didn't think he could be a good father either."

"*Was* he a good father?" she asked as calmly as she could, hardly able to believe he was talking like this.

"My grandfather was mean," he said through clenched teeth. "My dad was afraid he'd turn out the same. My grandfather always said my dad was just like him. But it was a lie. Most of what my grandfather said was a lie." His voice dropped. "But not about me."

"What did he say about you?" Dahlia frowned.

"My grandfather said I killed my sisters. And he was right, I did. I didn't mean to but I did." Arlen angrily dashed the wetness from his eyes. "I loved them more than anything, but I killed them. That's why my mother never wants me to come home."

She stared at him, too shocked to summon words that would help him. He stood alone, a solitary figure in his pain, until Glory called his name.

For the rest of the afternoon, Dahlia studied Arlen.

When Grant approached her later, she pulled him aside. "I think you need to talk to Arlen sooner rather than later, Grant," she whispered. "He just told me he thinks he's responsible for his sisters' deaths."

Every time she looked at him now she was reminded of their kiss. And every time she had to quash the yearning for more.

"That is serious." Surprised, Grant nodded. "I'll make it a point to talk to him as soon as I can."

She should be keeping her distance from Grant, but asking Grant to help her with Arlen would make keeping that distance impossible.

But she had to do it because together she and Grant could make a difference in the life of this boy who so touched her heart.

Chapter Eleven

Utterly and totally exhausted from the birthday party that was still going, and his attempts at a private chat with Arlen, which kept getting interrupted, Grant's hope of peace crashed when he remembered Kyle's turkey shoot. Dahlia, by contrast, looked ready for the next activity.

"How do you do it? You worked at the store, raced all over town with Arlen's treasure hunt, and yet you look like you just woke from an afternoon nap."

"Naps are for wimps," she said, wrinkling her nose.

A sound from the living room made him look past Dahlia to where the twins were opening their gifts from Dahlia. Glory was crying. He hurried over to comfort her, wondering at the cause.

"Look, Daddy." Glory said between sniffs.

"Dally gave us memory books just like the ones Mommy used to make."

"We miss Mommy," Grace wailed, tears rolling down her cheeks.

Very aware of Arlen and Dahlia watching him, Grant pulled out a tissue and dabbed at the tears on their cheeks.

"You don't talk about Mommy," Grace said, her voice slightly accusing.

Glory's clear blue eyes gazed into his. "Don't you miss Mommy?"

What could he say? That he hadn't talked about Eva because he didn't want to remember all he'd lost? Because he didn't want them to remember the wonderful life they'd had with her and realize he wasn't measuring up? Because he didn't want to cause them pain?

"Tell them," Dahlia whispered, stuffing more tissues into his hand. "They need to hear."

"I remember your mom, Glory. I don't think I'll ever forget her." Grant took Dahlia's advice and began to share memories he'd kept private until now.

"The first time I saw your mom she was playing with you two in the park. You were going down the slide and you, Glory, were scared. She kept telling you not to be afraid."

"I like slides," Glory said, her tears dissipating.

"You do now, because she taught you how to

go down, just like she taught you to try different things."

"Like pomegranates," Grace remembered. "Mommy got me to taste pomegranates."

"And onions," Glory added. Her nose wrinkled. "I don't like onions."

The other children loudly agreed.

"What else, Daddy?" Grace asked.

"I remember how your mom would hug you every night and put a special kiss on your forehead," he continued.

"I can't remember Mommy doing that." Glory's grin faded. "Why can't I remember, Daddy?"

Grant didn't have an answer to that. He felt every eye on him. The happiness on the twins' faces slowly faded and he knew it would only be moments until their tears returned. Why didn't he have the right words to say?

"Nobody remembers everything about the people who died." Arlen crouched down, his voice somber. "I can't remember everything about my sisters. But that doesn't mean I didn't love them or that they didn't love me."

Grace leaned her head on Arlen's shoulder. "How come?"

"Because people we love are tucked inside our hearts. Right here," he said, tapping his chest. "We can't remember everything, but every so often we remember something special like you did today when you opened those memory books. Maybe you can draw a picture in the book and that'll help you remember this birthday."

Glory looked at Grace. They nodded. Good humor restored, they thanked Dahlia for the books and the multicolored markers. "We like markers."

"I remember," Dahlia said with a chuckle.

Grant looked at her, suddenly recalling that first day on the train. He remembered seeing a yellow streak on the back of her jacket when they'd disembarked. Suddenly he knew the twins had a hand in making that yellow mark, though Dahlia had never said a word to him about it. What a lady.

"Do you want to open the rest of your gifts now?" The twins nodded, so Grant rose and moved out of the circle. Arlen followed. "Thank you," he said to the boy. "I appreciate you telling us about your sisters."

"You were right." Arlen followed him to the kitchen. "It does feel better to talk about my sisters. Maybe I'll tell you more someday."

"I'd be honored." Grant smiled, relieved that something had finally gotten through that tough shell. "Can you help the girls open the rest of their gifts now?"

Arlen nodded.

"You've had quite a day," Dahlia said, helping Grant restore the kitchen to order. "I wish he'd discuss his sisters more. I wonder what happened. He didn't tell you, did he?" She frowned when Grant shook his head.

"I think Glory is trying to find out." Grant lifted an eyebrow and tipped his head in the direction of the twins, who sat snuggled next to Arlen on the sofa. "Is it wrong to listen in?"

"Not when we're trying to help him." Dahlia set two chairs near the doorway, poured two cups of coffee and offered him one. Grant took it and sat beside her, very aware of her soft fragrance and the way her curls tumbled down her back. Sitting here beside her seemed so right. Then he heard Grace ask, "What were your sisters like, Arlen?"

Grant hoped the boy wouldn't brush off her question or hurt her feelings. He should have known better. Amusement threaded through Arlen's voice.

"Goofy. Just like you." He tweaked her pert nose. "Andrea and Priscilla loved to paint. They painted pictures of everything. I always gave them paints for their birthday and Christmas."

"Oh, no," Grant groaned in a whisper to Dahlia. "Now the twins will want to paint."

She smothered a laugh, her eyes dancing.

"Did you tell them bedtime stories?" Grace asked.

"All the time." His face looked vulnerable in the lamplight. "And they fell asleep in the middle of them, just like you do."

"And then they died," Glory said. "Like Mommy." Arlen nodded. "Did they get sick?"

"No." Arlen's voice tightened. "It was my fault."

"Why?" Glory asked.

"Because I didn't do my job and take care of them. I forgot because I was in a hurry."

"You forgot?" Grace touched his cheek, her voice very tender when he nodded. "That's okay. People forget lots of things. I forgot to tell Daddy I loved him last night."

A lump lodged in Grant's throat.

"I forgot to put the lid on Daddy's special pen," Glory added, not to be outdone by her sister. "Now it doesn't write anymore. That's my fault. But that's not like when your sisters went to heaven, is it?"

"Not quite." Arlen sounded as choked up as Grant felt. He glanced sideways and saw that Dahlia was also moved.

"Your sisters know you didn't mean to make a mistake." Grace tipped her head to one side. "One time, Glory hit me. I was mad, but Mommy told me that love forgives and that I should forgive Glory." She bent to look into his face. "That means I shouldn't be mad at her or blame her."

"I know." Arlen swallowed hard.

"It means you have to forgive *you*," Glory told him sternly.

"I'll try," Arlen promised, his voice choked.

A long silence stretched. Dahlia wiped a tear from her cheek, her smile tremulous. Grant couldn't take the tension any longer. He rose and stepped through the doorway. It was either that or kiss darling Dahlia again.

"I doubt if you two are hungry enough for a big supper," he said later. "How about I make cheese sandwiches?'

"Okay." Glory threw her arms around Arlen's neck. "And two for Arlen, 'cause he's big," she explained. "Dally, how many for you? Daddy makes them really good."

"He's a very special daddy, isn't he?" Dahlia smiled at Glory; then her gaze slipped to Grant. Her cheeks pinked. "And Arlen is your special friend. Do you know how lucky you girls are?"

"Yep!" They grinned at each other. A moment later they huddled together on the floor to reexamine their birthday gifts.

Grant was about to turn away and begin preparing the sandwiches. But he paused to watch Dahlia move into the living room as Arlen rose from the sofa. The boy towered over her, but she didn't look intimidated. She reached up and touched his shoulder.

"I wish I'd known your sisters, Arlen. They must have been special, too."

He nodded, easing away from her touch but saying nothing. Grant had a hunch he was still choked up.

"The twins are right." Earnestness filled Dahlia's voice. "Your sisters loved you. They'd understand a mistake, whatever it was. We all make them. I did, too."

"You? But you're always Miss Perfect." Arlen frowned. "What mistake did you make?"

"I wasn't there when my brother needed me," she told him. "I got sucked up in my own stuff and didn't notice that he was desperate for my help."

"What happened?"

Dahlia explained, but Grant could see the words cost her. Grant knew she was still trying to make up for not being there for her brother just as Arlen was still punishing himself for his sisters' deaths.

"But can *you* forgive yourself?" Arlen asked after a long pause.

"I know that's what he would have wanted so I'm trying," Dahlia replied.

"Is that why you're pushing this go-kart

thing? Because of your brother?" Arlen's question dared her to tell the truth.

"In a way." Dahlia's smile broke free, bringing Grant relief. "Partly it's to show my parents. They never thought I was strong enough to take his place."

"Why do you have to take his place? You have your own place." When she didn't answer, Arlen knelt down to talk to the girls.

Dahlia walked into the kitchen. She looked slightly dazed.

"Are you okay?" Grant asked.

"I'm not sure." She set napkins at each place, but her attention was elsewhere. "Did you hear what he said? He said I have my own place. I never thought of it like that before."

There were a hundred things Grant could have said to help her realize that she didn't have to earn anything, but he let her muse on it alone. Dahlia had spent a long time trying to make others proud of her, but what she really wanted was to be proud of the woman she was. He had a hunch that discovering that for herself would be a major milestone.

"Are the sandwiches ready, Daddy?" Glory tugged at his leg.

"Just about. You and Grace go and wash your hands." Grant flipped one sandwich, delighted when it landed perfectly in the pan.

"Daddy, look!" Grace squealed. "It's snowing."

Dahlia came back to life. She hurried to the window and peered outside. A groan seeped from her.

"Grace, will you ask Arlen to help you and your sister wash up?" He shut off the stove, waited until they were alone then walked over to Dahlia. "What is it? What's wrong?"

"I tried to tell you earlier. I got a letter from my mother today. They're going to come and visit to see the progress I've made." She gazed at him. She didn't need to say any more. He understood.

"You want to show them all you've done, to present a fait accompli," he guessed. "With the snow covering, you won't be able to do that."

"Because I haven't finished it, Grant. I've tried so hard but I just can't make it work."

"I know." He gathered her into his arms, pressed her head to her should and just held her as she wept.

A moment later they both heard the twins coming and Dahlia broke free of his embrace, dashing the tears from her eyes.

"Please excuse me," she said, her voice full of heartbreak. "I have to go."

Though the twins and Arlen tried to persuade her to stay and eat with them, Grant said nothing as he helped Dahlia pull on her jacket. She said a quick goodbye then hurried away, trudging through the wisps of white that now covered the ground, a small, lonely figure in the vast outdoors.

Arlen said nothing for a few moments. When they could no longer see her through the window he glanced at Grant. "She's upset the track isn't ready, isn't she?"

"Yes," Grant said then added, "Her parents are coming soon. It's a big deal to Dahlia to show them what she's accomplished. Without the karts running on the track…" He wanted Arlen to seriously consider what this failure of this project meant to Dahlia.

"She asked me to help and I wouldn't do it. I told her I was busy," Arlen admitted, "but that wasn't true."

"Then why did you say it?" Grant asked.

"Because I was mad at her," he admitted in a rueful voice. "She has everything. At least I thought she did. Everybody's making a big deal about her and this track and how she's pulling it all together and I thought, 'Why should I make it easy for her?'" Arlen shook his head. "I didn't realize the track was about her brother and her parents."

"And now that you do?" Grant slid the sandwiches onto a plate and set them on the table along with a gallon of milk.

"I dunno."

"You can still help. It's not too late. There are still the tires to be painted. There's lots left to do." Grant didn't want to press the boy. He wanted Arlen to *want* to help Dahlia, but all he could do now was pray for God to soften the boy's heart. As they ate, the twins asked Arlen if he'd help them build a snowman tomorrow. Arlen shook his head.

"Sorry. I can't. I think I'll be painting some tires tomorrow." He winked at Grant. "Laurel says the first snow in Churchill never stays."

"I sure hope she's right," Grant said with a grin.

Arlen babysat while Grant went to the turkey shoot. By the time he returned home, the boy was sacked out in the spare room, where he'd stay until Grant took him back to Lives in the morning.

With everyone asleep, Grant sat in his darkened living room and stared out at the whirling snow, which had kept some of the turkey shoot crowd home. He worried that they hadn't made enough to make Dahlia's dream come true.

Grant struggled to pray as Rick had directed him. In the past he'd always held some part of himself back. Now he tried to release his distrust in God, for Dahlia.

Please, please make the snow melt so she can have her dream. Please? She's worked so hard. Let her have that much.

This desperate craving to see Dahlia's dream realized was confusing for Grant. Though he wanted the best for Dahlia, he was no longer sure that completion of the track *was* the best thing for her. He desperately wanted her to be happy. Actually he wanted to be the one to make her happy.

It had felt so right to comfort her earlier, to be there to support and encourage her.

But Dahlia deserved a man who could love her and Grant didn't have the ability to do that.

But oh, how he wished he did.

On Thanksgiving Day, Grant squeezed his eyes closed as he held the phone and listened. He had a lot to be thankful for today.

"Dahlia and the boys are going to be so happy," he said into the phone. "Thank you. And happy Thanksgiving," he said.

For a few moments he hugged the secret information to himself, relishing the response he knew he'd get when he made it public. Mostly he relished the thrill of telling Dahlia.

Grant stepped out the back door to inhale

the crisp autumn air. The snow was long gone. Sunshine blazed across the land.

Dahlia. He could imagine the flash of gold that would shoot through her eyes before her dazzling smile appeared. He'd scarcely seen her since the twins' birthday, but that didn't matter. He just had to close his eyes and he could visualize her face. Somehow thoughts of her were always with him.

Grant had believed that keeping his distance would diminish his fascination with Dahlia, but he'd been so wrong.

Dahlia was embedded in every detail of his life. If he closed his eyes, he could breathe in her soft fragrance that reminded him of sunshine; he could hear her laughter. When his negative thoughts grew strong, he heard her voice chiding him to look on the positive side. The day dragged if Dahlia wasn't there to share it. It was Dahlia's smile he craved, Dahlia he wanted to be with.

What was this? Love?

No. Couldn't be. Grant was certain he was capable of feeling love again. So why was he so attracted to her? Dahlia hadn't coaxed him. By simply being herself, she'd become part of his life. Even if he wanted to, Grant couldn't forget her. Dahlia was unforgettable.

Confused, Grant went inside and poured himself another cup of coffee. Then he sank into his chair perched in the kitchen's sunniest spot.

Eva's Bible sat on a nearby stand. He'd planned to study the fragile onion-skin pages many times since her death to find answers and yet somehow he'd never gotten past the first page of Genesis. He felt so guilty every time he looked at it that he'd almost decided to put it away, store it for the girls.

But Grant needed somebody to talk to and according to Rick, God was the one with all the answers. So he picked up the Bible, held the covers between his hands and let the book fall open. The seventh chapter of Matthew.

If you, being evil, know how to give good gifts to your children, how much more will your Father in heaven give good things to those who ask Him?

Gifts. For their birthdays Grant had given the twins tiny silver lockets with their names engraved inside. He'd wanted something lasting to cherish, so they'd feel cared for. The girls had seemed thrilled.

This verse said that God was better at giving good gifts than Grant was. Did that mean God could give the gift of love to him?

At the service yesterday, Rick had said that God was the giver of good gifts, that, "it gives Him joy to see His kids smiling and happy."

Until Eva, Grant had never felt loved. He still didn't understand it. How did one get to love another? To have love grow inside *him*—it seemed impossible. All he wanted was to make sure Dahlia was happy. Was that love? Grant read the passage again.

I don't understand, God. Why would you love me? How can I be loved when I can't love?

For the first time since Eva's death, Grant examined their relationship, compared it to what he'd seen and heard among his new friends in Churchill and was stunned. His feelings for Eva had their basis in insecurity. They'd never had that sweet sharing of kindred souls. He'd accepted all Eva lavished on him. But what had he given back? He'd been so afraid to push past *his* needs, *his* fears, *his* problems to find out hers.

What a terrible deal Eva had made when she'd married him.

Grant glanced at himself in the mirror across the room and reminded himself that whatever he felt for Dahlia, he couldn't let anything come of it.

The doorbell rang.

"Hi, Rick. Come on in. I was just thinking of you."

"All good, I hope. Are you busy?" Rick followed him to the kitchen.

"The twins are at the hotel with Laurel and

Dahlia, making pies for the big Thanksgiving dinner tonight." He poured Rick a cup of coffee and freshened his own. "I'm supposed to go there to peel potatoes in an hour or so but I've got time to chat till then. What's up?"

"You're on potato detail, too, huh?" Rick chuckled.

"I just got a phone call from Kyle and thought I'd share with you. He's got the final tally on the turkey shoot. We did well." The figure Rick quoted made Grant's brows rise. "Think Dahlia's going to be happy?"

"If she isn't, my news should do it. I had a phone call from a man who's willing to donate his garage for as long as it takes the boys to get the go-karts running, *and* he's offered his expertise as a former mechanic." Grant high-fived Rick. "Now all we need is enough money to pay for transporting the go-karts from Thompson."

"Taken care of, pal. Laurel approached the government to cover transportation of the karts to Churchill as part of therapy for the boys. They agreed." Rick grinned. "God is really blessing Dahlia's idea. Now, if the weather holds until the karts are operational, it might all come together before a freeze up."

"God giving good gifts to His children," Grant murmured. Seeing Rick's quizzical look, he explained the verse he'd just read. "But why?

That's the thing that keeps stymieing me. Why would God love us so much?"

"Well, why do you love Grace and Glory?" Rick asked. "You're not related by blood. They must have made you change a lot of your life. As sweet as they are, I'm sure they aggravate you sometimes. So how can you love them?"

"I just do," Grant admitted, slightly surprised to realize how naturally those words came. "They're my kids."

"Same with God," Rick said. "Love is love. Giving of yourself, caring for someone else more than you care for you, being willing to let go of what you want most to make another happy—that's love. God gave it to us so we could enjoy each other. As much as we might think we must aggravate God by failing to understand His love, He doesn't give up. His very nature is love."

"And all we're supposed to do is accept it?" Grant felt stupid for asking, but he desperately needed to get this straight.

"Love is a verb. It *does*." Rick smiled. "Part of love is accepting it, but the most rewarding part of love is giving it." Rick raised an eyebrow. "What's troubling you?"

Grant needed to understand love as it pertained to a relationship with God. Maybe that would help him be the father God expected.

Maybe if he understood love, he could figure out his feelings for Dahlia.

So Grant asked all the questions about faith and fatherhood he'd never dared voice. At first he was embarrassed to show his ignorance, but Rick's explanation about God as a loving father helped Grant come to terms with his terrible memories of life with his father. He also understood why Eva's love had been the start of his healing.

Because Rick offered quiet understanding, Grant felt able to reveal the deep-seated fear he kept inside.

"What if I've inherited the abuse gene from my father?" He looked down, disgraced that he even needed to ask. "What if I end up hurting the girls."

"You haven't so far, have you?" Rick asked in a stern voice.

"No. And I don't ever intend to, but I do mess up, forget things, have a short temper." He couldn't look Rick in the eye. "I got angry at the twins the morning of their party."

"Why?"

"They spilled icing all over themselves, the kitchen and the floor."

"Did you hurt them or yell at them or make them cry?"

"No, but I scolded them," he admitted shame-faced.

"Because making a mess was something your father hated." Rick's gaze intensified.

"Yes. It was the same at Dahlia's when we were making cookies. Flour everywhere, cookie dough stuck on everything. I almost lost it."

"But you didn't lose it. You stuck it out." Rick shook his head. "That's the difference, Grant. That's why you'll never be an abuser. Abusers put themselves first and pretend it's for their kid. Real parenting is putting your kid's needs first and your own needs last. That's what you're doing."

"But it doesn't come automatically," Grant murmured in confusion.

"Why would you think it should?" Rick sounded amused. "You've never been a father before, have you? Or practiced on some other kid?"

Grant shook his head.

"Did you always know how to teach life skills?" Rick asked.

"I took lots of courses. But there's no manual for fatherhood. Everything is trial and error, and some of my errors might be bad for the twins."

"Then you'll apologize and do better."

"You don't understand," Grant muttered. "It's not that easy. I'm not like Dahlia. Parenting comes so easy to her. I just mentioned the twins' birthdays and she was full of ideas. I didn't have a clue where to start."

"Nobody said fatherhood was easy. And Dahlia is amazing, that's true." Rick smiled. "But God didn't make her responsible for the twins. He gave you that job."

"Exactly." Grant huffed out his frustration.

"You're questioning God's decision?" Rick grinned at Grant's chagrined look. "Parenting isn't a sure thing for anybody. Take me. Cassie eased into parenting her son, Noah, but I didn't. The day I married her I became Noah's father. No training. But I *am* his father and I have to do my best for him. So every day I pray for God's leading, do the best I can and leave the rest in God's hands."

"Maybe I need to buy another book on parenting," Grant mused.

"You already have the best one there is. The Bible." Rick's face sobered. "Study it. Check your ideas against what it says. Consult with other parents. But most of all, pray for guidance. God knows what you're going through. He's a father, too, and His kids get into far more trouble than yours."

Grant's watch alarm went off. "My cue to start peeling potatoes," he said.

"Mine, too." Rick zipped his jacket while

Grant pulled on his own. As they strode toward the hotel, Rick said, "If you ever want to talk again, I'm always available. Even if you only want to talk about Dahlia."

Grant stopped, paused then muttered, "What do you mean?"

"I mean your feelings for her. Buddy, I recognize the signs," Rick said when Grant would have argued. "You get the same goofy look I used to get when I met Cassie. You care about Dahlia, don't you?"

"Yes," Grant admitted. "But I'm not sure what that means."

"Can I offer some advice?" He waited for Grant's nod. "Dahlia has convinced herself she must manage on her own. She believes her project will show her competence, so she won't deviate from her goal no matter what it costs her."

"I know," Grant agreed. "That's why we've got to make her project succeed."

"My advice to you is, support her as best you can while helping her see that her competence doesn't come from what she accomplishes. It comes from who she is, a woman who has God on her side." Rick nodded. "That's the most powerful help any of us have."

Though he'd never especially enjoyed peeling potatoes, Grant walked inside the hotel with excitement building inside. Because this was for

Dahlia, potato peeling had gone from being a chore to being a pleasure.

Was that what Rick had been talking about when he said those things about doing stuff for others? Because if it was, Grant would do a lot more than peel potatoes for the lovely Dahlia.

Chapter Twelve

On a Friday afternoon two weeks after Thanksgiving, Dahlia drove to Lives to ask Arlen for help. The trip was not a success.

"I painted the tires, but I'm too busy to help with the garage," he snapped.

"It's not hard work." Dahlia frowned at the anger in Arlen's voice. He'd put up barriers between them again. "The other boys have helped organize the shelves. I thought you might help me fill them. It won't take long."

"I said no!" The sharp response had barely left his lips when Arlen flushed. "Sorry, but I can't," he said in a quieter voice. "I'm tied up."

The way he said it made Dahlia frown.

"You don't have to look so suspicious," he said. "It's nothing bad."

"I'm sure it isn't. Thanks anyway." Dahlia conceded defeat as he sauntered away.

Two minutes later, the other boys rushed outside, eager to begin preparing the area Kyle would soon flood to make an outside hockey rink. Temperatures had dropped considerably in the past few days and now the frost took till late morning to dissipate. The signs were all there. Winter was coming.

Plagued by a sense of urgency to get the go-karts on the track at least once before the land was obliterated by snow, Dahlia couldn't rest. She pushed through her days at the store, desperate to steal every moment to work on another project detail.

A new missive from her mother suggested her parents' visit could happen any day. If they appeared, what would she have to show? A project half-finished?

She was reaching into the hall closet when she heard Arlen speaking in the next room.

"Hey, Rod. I just got a call," Arlen said.

"Oh. From who?"

"My probation officer. My mom's decided she won't make me a ward of the court. She wants me back."

Dahlia shook herself out of her trance and walked quickly toward the kitchen, anxious that Arlen not think she was spying on him. She sat there for a long time, stunned, trying to absorb the news that would certainly put an end to her plan to adopt.

"Hello. Come to join me for coffee?" Laurel poured two cups of coffee and handed one to Dahlia. "You look upset. Can I help?"

"Uh, I was trying to persuade Arlen to help me, but he says he's too busy."

"He's been meeting with Grant. I understand there's some homework involved."

"Oh, that explains it. I hope it helps him." She sighed. "I have to get this project finished, especially now."

"Why especially now?" Laurel asked.

"My parents are coming. I don't have a firm date, but knowing them, they'll arrive without notice." She made a face. "I sound like a whiner. Ignore me. I'm just concerned. The Weather Channel is predicting snow by the weekend."

"Which isn't unusual," Laurel reminded. "Sweetie, you always knew there was a risk you wouldn't finish before the snow arrived."

"But I've prayed so hard. We're so close." Dahlia forced a smile. "Why can't I get this done?"

"God's still in control though He may not do things the way you want." Laurel grinned. "Want proof? The karts will be on tomorrow's train and we won't have to pay a dime."

"Really?" A weight lifted off Dahlia's shoulders. *Thank You, Lord.* "I can't thank you enough for going to bat for us, Laurel."

"You're doing this for my boys. Of course I'll help." Laurel studied her. "But I get the feeling there's more on your mind."

"I feel like a failure," Dahlia admitted.

"Then, girl, you need to take a walk over that track again."

"I overheard Arlen talking to Rod," Dahlia admitted. "Is it true his mom rescinded her decision to make him a ward of the court?"

"It's true." Laurel's forehead furrowed. "She wants him to come home when his sentence here is finished, to try to rebuild their relationship. Arlen's all she has left now."

With those few words, Dahlia's dream to shower Arlen with the love she'd stored inside melted into ashes.

"I'm sorry, honey. But you'll be a mom in God's time." Laurel hugged her.

That tenderness was her undoing. Dahlia couldn't stem her tears.

"Why am I never enough, Laurel? What's wrong with me?"

"Nothing!" Laurel exclaimed. "It's just—I guess God has a different plan."

"So what is it? I've tried so hard to prove myself. And yet I keep failing." The lump in her throat blocked the rest of Dahlia's words.

"That's a lie." Grant stood in the doorway. His face flushed a rich red when Dahlia turned to him. "I didn't mean to listen in, but I have to say this." His gray gaze searched hers. "You haven't failed, Dahlia. You've achieved a lot. The go-karts are arriving. That's an answer to prayer."

"And if we need extra money to fix them? I will *not* go back to this community. They've already given so much."

"You're jumping the gun," he said, his voice gentle.

"I'm trying to be prepared," she shot back.

"Are you?" He sat down as Laurel quietly slipped from the room. "There's a verse I found. It says, 'Sufficient unto the day is the evil thereof.' In other words, let tomorrow take care of itself. Jesus said the same thing when he was talking about the birds, remember?"

"I'm responsible if this thing falls apart."

"Why just you?" Grant said, surprising her. "We're all involved in this project, Dahlia. We've set up fund-raising, coaxed donations and talked about it nonstop. If it fails, it will be our faults, too." He arched an eyebrow. "Aren't you the one who keeps saying this is a *community* project?"

"Wow! You sound different." She saw a new confidence in his eyes.

"I'm learning who's in control." Grant stretched out his legs and leaned back, fingers meshed behind his head. "It isn't me and it's sure not you."

She kept her hands folded in her lap, wondering what had changed Grant.

"I believe God places things on our hearts that lead us to our goals. But just because our goals are directed by God doesn't mean we automatically get them. That'd be too easy."

"I wouldn't mind having things go easy with this project."

"I doubt you'd feel the same sense of accomplishment."

"So fighting through the problems is supposed to make me feel better?" She used her driest tone.

"Maybe it's supposed to make you question whether this is a worthy goal or simply an idea you aren't willing to pursue if the going gets tough," he suggested.

Dahlia studied him. "Any personal examples?"

"Not that I want to share right now."

Grant's words suggested a change in his faith. She wanted to know more and it seemed she would when he asked, "Will you come for dinner this evening?"

A faint smile shaped his lips. Dahlia remembered vividly what those lips had felt like on hers. Her heart began to race.

"I'd love to," she said without thinking, then realized it was true. "Can I bring anything?"

"Just yourself. Around six-thirty?" he asked.

"Sounds good."

"Okay. See you then." Grant rose, zipped up his jacket and grinned. "The twins are at story time so I'll use this hour to talk to the boys."

"What's today's discussion about?" she asked curiously.

"How striving to reach a goal teaches patience and purpose and a whole lot of other things we need to get what we most want out of life. That 'easy come' usually also means 'easy go.'" He arched an eyebrow. "See you later?"

"For sure." She watched him leave, noting a new assurance in the way he moved. Something had changed in Grant's world, and she couldn't wait to find out what it was.

Grant checked the oven for the tenth time. Everything looked good.

"I'm hungry, Daddy." Glory's plaintive voice joined Grace's just before the doorbell rang. "It's Dally!" they yelled as they raced toward the door.

"Hello, darlings." Dahlia scooped the girls

into her arms, then leaned back to study them. "You look so pretty."

"Daddy got us new dresses." Grace twirled around so her flouncy skirt flared. Of course, Glory followed. "I like pink and Glory likes yellow."

"You both look beautiful." Dahlia lifted her lovely hazel eyes and smiled so warmly Grant couldn't look away. "I'm so sorry I'm late. My parents phoned as I was leaving."

She let him help her with her coat and his breath vanished. Dahlia looked like a queen in her black velvet pantsuit trimmed with satin piping. Her hair, ablaze in a cloud of auburn curls, tumbled from its updo to caress her pale neck.

"You look lovely," he said truthfully. "What did your parents say?"

"Not much. They've decided to go on a cruise. They've set a tentative date for their visit. A month from last Monday." Dahlia's irrepressible smile blazed. "I've got until then to get the track finished."

"Prayer works." Grant smiled and refused her offer of help in the kitchen. "Dinner will be ready shortly. Till then, you can relax."

The twins took that as carte blanche to get Dahlia into one of their favorite word games, leaving Grant to admire the three auburn heads bent close together, giggling as they built words on the game board. He'd have to thank Rick for his advice to show Dahlia he was no longer the man she'd first met. Tonight, Grant intended her to see him in a different light: as a competent and confident father.

Maybe then—he didn't allow himself to finish that thought.

Sufficient unto the day, he repeated mentally as he stirred the gravy. Tonight was also about building Dahlia's confidence because he sensed she'd begun to give up on her dream.

When dinner was ready, Grant could have called them to the table, but he let them play on, content to admire the tender way Dahlia coaxed the twins to do better. Did she recognize the gift she had for helping people be more than they thought they could be? For the hundredth time Grant thought what a wonderful mother she'd make.

"Are we holding you up?" She tilted her head, catching him watching her.

"I thought I'd let you finish your game. Nothing will spoil."

Grace pounced when Dahlia wasn't looking. "S-i-g-n, sign," she said with a big grin. "I win."

"That's a very good word. You do win." Dahlia pressed a kiss on her forehead then glanced at Grant. "Shall we come to the table now?"

Grant held her chair, then helped the twins tie on polka-dot aprons. "Ready, girls?" he asked.

They could hardly wait to show off. A burst of pride shot through him as they carried the rolls and salad to the table.

"Good job," he cheered. "Now the potatoes and the vegetables. Okay?"

"We can do it, Daddy." Their voices brimmed with confidence.

"Yes, you can." When they finished their tasks, he helped them climb onto their chairs then he carried in the meat and the gravy. "Okay, we're all ready."

"It smells delicious." Dahlia's smile made his heart race.

"Enjoy." *I made it especially for you.* "Shall we say grace?"

The twins clasped each other's hands. When Dahlia slid her smooth palm into his, Grant's breath caught in his throat again. The twins recited a poem of thanks. Her delicate perfume assailed him, sending him into a dream world where dinners with her happened every day. When he opened his eyes, he found them all staring at him.

"Amen." He tucked away the dream. "Enjoy."

It was the kind of family meal Grant had imagined having when he was a boy. He wanted it to last forever.

"Can we have our special dessert now, Daddy?" Glory asked when they'd all finished the main course.

"It's special because we all made it together," Grace told Dahlia with a proud smile.

"Then I'll love it." Dahlia's smile echoed in her hazel eyes. Grant felt trapped in her smile and loved it. The very last thing he wanted was to move.

"I'll clear the table."

He couldn't allow that. "Stay put. You're our guest." He glanced at the girls and they began removing dishes from the table.

Dahlia watched them walk away. "You're doing an amazing job."

"Thanks. Coming here has been great for them." *And me.*

The sound of a dish hitting the floor broke the mood.

"Excuse me." Grant caught the flicker of worry in Dahlia's eyes and knew she was remembering his unease the day they'd made cookies.

But all she said was, "Of course."

Grant walked to the kitchen, steeling himself for the mess. The old rush of irritation building inside vanished when he saw Glory on the floor, holding her bleeding finger.

"Let's see." He tenderly examined her hand.

"It's not too bad, sweetie. We'll put on one of those funny bandages you like."

"But we made a mess, Daddy." Grace's face wrinkled as if she'd burst into tears.

"You sure did. But sometimes messes happen. So we clean them up." He smiled at her. "Right?"

"Right," she agreed, happy—and perhaps relieved?

"Why don't you go keep Dahlia company? After I fix Glory's finger, I'll clean this up."

Maybe he'd been wrong to give the two so much responsibility. But on the heels of that worry came the reminder that parenting was trial and error. He refused to allow the rush of guilt looming inside to overwhelm him.

"Okay, Daddy." Grace skipped to the doorway. "We made a mess, but Daddy's going to fix it," she announced.

Daddy's going to fix it. And that was the sum total of his job, Grant mused as he lifted Glory in his arms and carried her to the bathroom. As long as he kept fixing their world, he would do all right.

It didn't take long to bandage Glory's finger. He sent her back to the table while he cleaned up the kitchen, only then remembering that the apple Betty was still in the oven.

"I'm sorry," he muttered, carrying the too-crisp confection with its blackened edges to the table. "I left it in too long." He felt like a fool for trying to show off. He'd wanted Dahlia to see that he'd changed, but that seemed like a dumb idea now.

"It smells amazing. Do you have any ice cream?" she asked.

Grant nodded. His heart bumped at her sweet smile, erasing the doubt he'd been feeling just moments earlier.

"Everything tastes better with ice cream," she said cheerfully. "May I serve while you get it?"

"Sure." Grant went to search the freezer. He returned with a half-full container. "All we have is maple walnut," he said apologetically.

"Walnuts and maple are perfect with apples." She placed a scoop of ice cream on each serving of apples from which the blackened edge had been removed. "Doesn't that make your mouth water, girls?"

Grace and Glory nodded, eyes wide. They tasted, then grinned.

"It's really good, Daddy," Glory told him.

"It's a com—com—" Grace frowned. "I can't remember the word."

"What does the word mean, Grace?" Dahlia asked.

"That we all did it together."

"Community?" Dahlia smiled.

"That's it." Grace's face lit up. "This is a community dessert."

"Yes, it is," Grant agreed.

Grant couldn't stop staring at Dahlia, wondering whether there was a way in which they could be more than just friends. And for once, that wish had nothing to do with the twins.

"They're so adorable." Dahlia accepted the cup of tea Grant poured for her now that the twins were in bed. "I see a big change since I first met them on the train. They're calmer."

"I'm not sure about that." He sat down opposite her. "But I agree they seem more secure."

"That's due to you," she said quietly. Her eyes met his. "You've changed, too."

"I still have my moments," he told her.

"Everyone does." She debated a moment before asking what was on her mind. "Do you still feel you're failing Eva?"

"Yes, but life goes on. I'm responsible for the twins. I do my best. If I mess up, I try to make it right." He shook his head. "I know you've been telling me that for a while, but I had to figure it out for myself."

"How did you?" She couldn't conceal her curiosity.

"You helped me see there is no right way to parent, though I guess I had to hear it again from Rick to have it sink in. I do what I can and keep praying for help." Grant shrugged. "I still doubt every decision I make. I probably always will. But that isn't going to keep me from acting."

"Good for you." Dahlia smiled at him. "I think Eva would be proud." After a moment she said, "It's hard to go on without someone you loved."

After a pause he said, "It's getting easier."

"But?" Dahlia heard an unfinished note in his voice.

"I'm not a person who knows much about love, Dahlia."

"I don't understand." Dahlia wondered at the strain underlying his words.

"Love is practically a foreign concept to me," he explained. "My mom left when I was very young. My dad was— He wasn't a loving man. He was probably angry because she left me behind, but I've stopped making excuses for his behavior."

"He was abusive?" Dahlia's heart sank as his expression confirmed it. "I'm so sorry you had to go through that, Grant."

She reached across the table and squeezed his hand. Tension shifted the lines on his face as he fought his past.

"My father demanded more than any kid

should have to give and he took without ever saying thank you. He treated me like a servant. I doubt he even noticed when I left."

No wonder he'd struggled with fatherhood.

The desolate remark reached straight into Dahlia's heart, especially when he looked straight at her.

"There's nothing I wouldn't do for the twins. Why didn't he feel like that about me? How did I alienate him?"

Dahlia set her cup down and moved her chair next to his. She slid her arm around his shoulder. "You have to know it wasn't you."

"My head knows it, but—" He gave her a wry smile.

"Your father's problems had nothing to do with you, Grant. Maybe no one ever loved him the way he yearned to be loved."

Grant lifted his head. "I never thought of that."

"Perhaps your father never had anyone tell him he was worthwhile or that he mattered." Suddenly unnerved by her proximity to him, she eased her arm away and immediately regretted the loss of contact. "What about your mother?"

"I looked for her years ago. She died of cancer within a year of leaving my father. Maybe she needed to get away to die in peace."

"It's odd how everything in our lives always harks back to our childhood," Dahlia mused.

"Eva said our minds are molded in those tender years," he murmured. A half smile tugged at his lips. "I once told her I never wanted to be responsible for anyone else, that I wouldn't marry because I couldn't be a family man."

"You didn't want more children?" Dahlia hid her surprise. "What did Eva say?"

"She said nothing was ever so bad it couldn't be changed by love. She kept saying she loved me." He glanced down at their entwined fingers. "In hindsight, I was dependent on Eva. I'm not sure I gave as much as I got," he admitted. "Eva made it comfortable for me to remain aloof from everything. She bore the load in our relationship. She should have demanded more of me. She deserved more." His fingers tightened on hers.

"I never realized how little I gave back until I noticed the couples around here. They depend on each other. In order to work, their relationship needs both of them fully participating."

Dahlia nodded.

"I never knew caring about someone could be so demanding yet so fulfilling." His gray gaze met hers.

"You sound as if you've now found someone else to love." A shaft panic ripped through her when he slowly nodded. Who had Grant found to love?

"The twins, of course." Grant grinned and she grinned back as relief flooded through her. He hadn't found a mom for the twins. Yet. "I know it's not romantic, but I'd do anything to keep them safe and happy. In fact, that's my new goal."

"You've given up on finding a mother for them?"

"Maybe loving the twins is the only kind of love I can have." Grant looked down. "Maybe I'm not capable of the kind of love others experience."

"I don't believe that," Dahlia told him firmly. "I think God wants His children to experience all the shades of love He created."

"Maybe." Grant eased his hand from hers and leaned back in his chair. "When I first started speaking to Rick a couple of weeks ago, he recited a verse to me that's echoed in my head ever since. 'God hasn't given us a spirit of fear, but of love and of power and of a sound mind.'"

"It's a good one."

"Rick told me that if I put that verse in the boys' vernacular, it would be, 'God didn't create any dummies.'" He chuckled. "I repeat that when I'm fighting my spirit of fear."

While Grant sat in silent contemplation, self-truth filled Dahlia.

She loved Grant.

She hadn't tried very hard to find a mother for the girls because *she* wanted to be the woman in Grant's life. She wanted to tell him her secret fears and desires, and hear his. She wanted to be by his side to help raise the twins.

But that dream was impossible. She wasn't strong enough to be a wife or a mother. Maybe that's why Grant no longer saw her as a viable partner. Maybe that's why God hadn't answered her prayer about Arlen—because she didn't deserve those blessings.

She rose, hating to leave but she needed to get away and think about this.

"Thank you for a wonderful evening. You've come a long way from the dad who couldn't relate to his twins, Grant."

He rose to see her out. "Thanks, Dahlia."

A longing to share the burgeoning feelings in her heart swelled. Impulse overcame wisdom and without thinking, she leaned forward, touching her lips to his. After a momentary hesitation, Grant responded, deepening the kiss as he wrapped his arms around her.

This was what she wanted, to be with Grant like this. She wanted to share his hopes and dreams, and his fears. To be there for him.

And yet, she couldn't help it—doubts and worries flooded in. A moment later, as if Grant understood, he ended the embrace, his eyes searching hers as he stepped away.

"Thank you for coming," he said as he led her to the door and held her coat. Then, he pulled her back into his arms. "Don't you dare give up, Dahlia," he whispered.

She wasn't exactly sure what he meant but in the moment, she didn't have the strength to ask. It was enough to relish the joy of being in Grant's arms for the second time that night.

"Good night" was the best she could manage when she finally eased free of his embrace.

She drove home with her brain whirling with questions, her lips still tingling from that wonderful kiss.

Chapter Thirteen

On November 11th, after the Remembrance Day ceremony was finished, Grant walked into the garage and saw Dahlia dressed in shabby jeans, a red plaid shirt and boots that were clearly too big. He didn't bother to stifle his laughter.

"Are you really laughing at me, Grant Adams?"

"Actually—yes." He chuckled harder at the fierce frown she shot his way. "How much do you actually know about mechanics?" he asked, shedding his coat on a nearby box.

"Less than you, probably." Dahlia's indomitable smile appeared as she shrugged. "They've almost fixed this kart. Maybe we can try it on the track soon."

She looked so cute with that streak of grease on the end of her nose, her fist clenched around a massive wrench. Grant couldn't stop staring at her.

"I keep trying to tell her there's no such thing as almost fixed." Pete, the mechanic who was helping the boys repair the go-karts, winked at Grant. "You'd better take that away from her. She could do herself an injury."

"You know me better than that, Pete." Dahlia gave him a mock glare.

"I know saying you can't do something is like waving a red flag in front of a bull, Dahlia Wheatley. But the boys and I need peace and quiet, and you're hovering." Pete pretended a glare. "Why don't you two go do something fun and leave us to work?"

"But I want to help," she argued.

"You'll be a bigger help if you leave us in peace," he said. An amused rumble of agreement came from the three boys beside him.

"I will be back," Dahlia assured him before she turned to Grant. "Want to go to the track? We could check that everything's good to go."

"I know very well that you did that yesterday, and the day before, and the day before that." It was a token objection because Grant knew he was happy to do whatever she wanted. "Okay, we'll go to the track if you want, but I'm not anxious to take the girls. There were two sightings of polar bears yesterday."

"Arlen's babysitting, isn't he?" Grant nodded. "So we'll take him along. You know you can trust him to keep an eye on the girls."

Grant remembered Rick's verse. *God has not given us a spirit of fear.*

"Hardly seems like rain, doesn't it? But that's what the weatherman predicts," Dahlia said as they got in his truck and headed toward Grant's.

"They're never right," Grant said, then wished he hadn't in case he'd raised Dahlia's hopes. He figured getting her project operational before winter hit wasn't likely, though he'd never say that out loud. "The ugly weather has to come sooner or later."

"Later is fine." She pulled into his yard. "Usually I love winter, but putting out sleds for the kids and snow-blowers for their parents at the store just isn't doing it for me this year."

"Dahlia, can we talk about that kiss?" Grant blurted and held his breath when her lovely hazel eyes stretched wide.

"Uh, okay." Her cheeks pinked when she glanced at him before quickly averting her face.

That was it? Grant shifted awkwardly, waiting, hoping she'd say something, anything more. She didn't.

"Why did you kiss me, Dahlia?" he asked finally, frustrated by her continued silence.

"I probably shouldn't have." She kept staring straight ahead.

"So why did you?" He desperately wanted to know what that gesture of hers meant, especially if their embrace had meant as much to her as it had to him.

"I guess I wanted to show you I cared," she mumbled.

"Cared?" He seized on the word. "Cared how?"

"You were hurting," she said. "You'd just told me about your dad and I..."

"You felt sorry for me?" Grant almost groaned. He so did not want her pity.

"It was more than pity." She did glance at him then. Her hazel eyes held a message that Grant couldn't decipher before she demanded, "Why did you kiss me back?"

"I—uh—you were—" he stammered to a stop while his brain searched for an answer.

Oh, why had he ever started this? His brain was so jumbled, his emotions all over the place. On top of that, he didn't want to say something without thinking it over carefully lest he later regret it. Most of all, he didn't want to hurt Dahlia in any way.

Relief flooded him when Grace peeked out the front door and waved them inside.

"Maybe we should continue this later," he suggested, seizing on the excuse.

"Sure," Dahlia hurriedly agreed. "Anyway, I have to focus on finishing my project."

She sounded like she was also glad for the reprieve that meant she didn't have to answer. Suddenly Grant wished that the track was finished, the karts were operational and she was finally free of the worry that dogged her.

Let her get one kart around that track, Grant prayed as he opened his door. *Just one. Please?* When had Dahlia's project become so important to him?

Since she'd taken over his world.

"It looks pretty good, don't you think?" Dahlia snugged her collar around her ears, turning her back on the wind that raced across the land.

"It looks ready." Grant smiled as the twins squealed in a game of tag with Arlen. "There's nothing more to do. It's waiting for a go-kart."

"I can't thank you enough for all you've done. This wouldn't have happened without you." She felt so close to him. If only she could have told him what was in her heart when he asked about that kiss. "I wish—"

She heard a noise before the wind caught it and tossed it away. When she turned to look, Dahlia's blood froze.

"Grant," she hissed, grabbing his hand.

"I see it. So do the kids." He raised his voice a

notch. "Don't move, guys." They both watched as a polar bear waddled near Arlen and the twins. "Let's move toward them very slowly." Grant's voice was hoarse.

They inched forward together. The closer they got, the more clearly Dahlia heard the twins' whimpers. She could also hear the bear's low-throated growl.

"No way," Arlen repeated, fiercely trying to stay between the bear and the girls. "You're not getting near them."

But the hungry bear knew how to maneuver.

"Get out of here!" Arlen suddenly yelled, flailing his arms. The bear backed off only for a moment, then shifted closer to Glory.

"What do we do, Grant?" Dahlia breathed.

"Don't make any sudden moves," he said. "We don't want to force it into defense mode. Ease up, Arlen," he said a little louder. "Keep calm, girls. Daddy's here."

Daddy's here. If Grant could only hear himself, he'd never doubt his abilities again.

Please help us, Lord. The repeated prayer left her lips over and over.

Grant moved cautiously but unerringly closer to the twins. He was steps away when the bear suddenly lunged. With lightning speed, Arlen stepped in front of Glory and swung his arm to swat away the bear's paw. But the claws sunk into his arm.

Arlen screamed with pain while Grant and Dahlia raced toward him and the twins. She grabbed the twins' hands and pulled them toward the truck. With the girls safely inside, she turned back to see what else she could do. Arlen was on the ground, clutching his injured arm. Grant stood in front of the snarling bear, yelling. He used a broken tree branch as a club, swinging it at the lunging bear.

"Daddy!" Glory's whimper forced Dahlia into action.

She started the truck, threw it into gear and raced toward Grant while honking the horn. While the bear was distracted Grant scored a direct hit to the bear's head and the animal backed off, but its eyes returned to Arlen, who was still on the ground.

Behind her, the twins whimpered. Dahlia hit the gas as Grant moved between Arlen and the bear. She pulled up and leaned over to thrust open the passenger door.

"Get in!" she yelled before hitting the horn again.

The bear stood fully upright, preparing to attack.

Dazed and bleeding, Arlen staggered to his feet. Grant thrust one arm around his shoulders and half dragged the boy to the truck. He boosted him inside and jumped in, too. As soon as the door closed, Dahlia backed away and took off.

Dahlia called the police, knowing that they would call the wildlife service. Then she called Laurel.

"There's a bear inside the fence. Keep everyone indoors until you hear otherwise," Dahlia told her friend what had happened. "We're taking Arlen to the hospital."

Laurel promised to meet them there. Dahlia hit the gas and raced to the emergency room.

"I think he's in shock," she explained to the attendants who hurried Arlen away as soon as they got him out of the car.

Grant shot her a questioning glance. She could see he needed to make certain Arlen was okay. She guessed he felt a bit of guilt because Arlen had been injured protecting his children.

"Go with him," she urged, feeling queasy. "I'll take care of the twins."

Dahlia led the girls to the waiting room and spent some time reassuring them that Arlen would be okay. A few moments later, Laurel appeared.

"Arlen?" she asked breathlessly.

"Grant's with him now." Dahlia glanced at the twins. "Arlen was a hero today." She shuddered at the thought of what could have happened.

"The area is fenced to stop this exact thing." Laurel was visibly upset. "I'll get Kyle to check the perimeter before anyone goes on the track again."

"Let the wildlife people do that." Dahlia realized she was still trembling.

"You two are okay?" Laurel asked the twins, who clutched one another, tear marks still on their cheeks. Glory and Grace nodded.

"Daddy and Arlen saved us," Grace said, her voice shaky.

"That's because they love you," Laurel said, hugging them. "I'm going to check on Arlen now. Will you pray for him?"

As Laurel left, both girls bowed their heads About to join them, Dahlia found she couldn't say a word. Grant had left his jacket on a nearby chair, and one sleeve was ripped. There was a large red stain around the tear.

Her heart squeezed so tight it hurt. Had the bear injured him, too? Had the doctors noticed? Were they treating him?

Oh, God, please, please don't let Grant be hurt. Because I love him.

"I'm very grateful for what you did, Arlen," Grant said in a gruff tone, unable to hide his relief.

"Twenty-two stitches isn't much," the boy bragged, glancing at his bandaged arm.

Dahlia smiled, but Grant couldn't. Not yet.

"You saved my kids' lives. Thank you," he said.

Arlen nodded and grabbed another slice of Polar Bear Pizza.

It had been Dahlia's idea to come here once the doctor had released Arlen. Grant had agreed. They needed time to relax, let the fear die down in a place away from the tense atmosphere at the hospital before the twins tried to sleep. To reassure himself, he took a second glance at the pair. They sat silent, watching Arlen, their eyes wide with fear still clinging to the depths.

"They're fine, Grant," Dahlia assured him softly. "And thank God, so are you. That blood on your jacket scared the daylights out of me."

"It was just a scratch," he assured her for the tenth time. "Nothing to worry about."

Her eyes met his. "I do worry about you, Grant. All the time." Then she shyly broke the connection.

Grant loved her concern for him. For just a moment he wished he had been injured enough that she'd fling her arms around him so he could feel Dahlia's embrace again and savor the sweet caring she'd lavished on him at the hospital, until the doctors had reassured her he wasn't injured.

Glory nestled against Arlen's good arm, as if to reassure herself that he was all right. Arlen patted her shoulder. A moment later Grace copied her sister, snuggling next to the boy.

"Why did you jump in front of the bear, Arlen?" Grace's blue eyes gazed at him with adoration. "You got hurt."

"Your dad was too far away," Arlen explained. "I knew he couldn't get there fast enough. I couldn't let that bear near you." He smiled and tickled her under the chin.

"He could have eaten us," Grace said in a whisper.

"Nope. You and Glory are too small to make a good bear dinner," he insisted.

"But your arm's hurt," Grace said.

"I'll be fine, I promise," he told the girls.

Grace peered up at him. "Did you save your sisters like that?"

"No." Arlen fell silent, staring at his food.

It seemed the twins understood his silence, for they simply rested against him. Then Glory soberly invited him to play with them.

"Maybe later." His smile didn't reach his eyes. "After I finish my pizza. But you two should build a tower with those awesome blocks. I'd like to see that."

They checked to be sure he was serious then nodded and, holding hands, walked to the toy area. "Will you tell us what happened to your sisters, Arlen?" Dahlia rested her hand on his arm. "It might help to talk about it."

Arlen studied her for a long time. But Grant saw no malevolence in his gaze, just inexpressible sadness.

"You can tell us," Grant urged.

Arlen finally nodded.

"We were going on a picnic." He pushed away his plate and leaned back against the seat. "Mom said I could fish. She only had a few hours off until she had to go back to work the late shift at the diner so we were hurrying, me most of all because I loved fishing and I could almost feel them nibbling on my line. It was one of those perfect summer days when it seems like nothing can go wrong." His voice cracked.

Grant noticed that Dahlia's eyes were already brimming with tears.

"I rushed my sisters into the car and told them to do up their seat belts while I got my tackle and stowed it in the trunk. I got in the front seat. I remember asking them if their belts were on," he said, then paused, his throat working as he fought to regain control of his emotions. "They said yes. Then Mom got in and we took off."

His voice cracked and he stopped. Under the

table, Grant slid his hand into Dahlia's and held on. Neither of them said a word. This was Arlen's moment. They waited for him to regain his composure.

"We'd only gone a block when a truck ran a stop sign and hit us. My sisters were thrown from the car." He gulped. Tears coursed down his cheeks. "They died and it was my fault."

"Oh, honey, how could it be your fault?" Dahlia whispered.

"I should have known their belts weren't fully latched. It happened before. I should have known to check even though they said they'd fastened them." He dashed the back of his hand across his face to obliterate his tears.

"Arlen, sweetie—" Grant loved the tenderness in Dahlia's voice.

"It *was* my fault. My mother said it over and over."

"Oh, sweetie." Dahlia reached out and touched his cheek. "Your mom needed to lash out at someone in her grief. She didn't mean it. It's just something she said in the heat of the moment."

"No." He shook his head. "After the funeral she told me she never wanted to see me again. She hates me. I hate myself!" He jumped up and rushed outside. The twins noticed and rose, frowning.

"Can you get the girls home and to bed,

Dahlia?" Grant asked. "I need to talk to him, to help him deal with his feelings."

"Of course. The twins will be fine." She pressed his arm when he hesitated. "Go, Grant. He needs you and you can help him."

"Thank you." He squeezed her shoulder, and in a rush of understanding, he now knew the feeling hidden inside him was love.

Love for this wonderful woman.

He grabbed his tattered jacket and shrugged into it. As he pushed through the door into the pouring rain, Grant suddenly stopped.

What would he do when Dahlia found someone special to fill her life with? When he had to manage on his own without her behind him, backing him, supporting him?

Then Grant knew the truth.

He couldn't let that happen.

Somehow, someway, Grant had to keep Dahlia Wheatley in his life.

Permanently.

"Give me the right words for Arlen, Lord. And about Dahlia..." He let his heart speak for him, knowing God would understand.

Chapter Fourteen

"Thank heaven the rain has stopped." Dahlia rang up Grant's purchase order for the sleds he'd chosen for the twins for Christmas.

"When she offered me a job, Laurel never said anything about a rainy season. I think my house might float away if it continues," Grant teased with a smile.

"It's not normal for Churchill to have rain at the end of November, especially so much of it," Dahlia assured him. "Climate change I guess."

"There is a lot of water." Grant's smile bathed her in comforting warmth but it couldn't dispel the urgency she felt to get the project completed. "I guess it'll eventually sink in."

"All I need is one nice warm day to dry off the track. Then we can get a kart on it. It's not for me," Dahlia defended when he grinned. "Everyone who has contributed to the project needs to see results for all their fund-raising efforts."

Grant didn't say anything as she handed him back his credit card. His odd expression confused her. Why did he keep staring? She reached up and patted the combs that held her curls in place. Grant's steady regard was scrambling her train of thought.

"I never did get a chance to ask you about your talk with Arlen," she said. "How did it go?"

"He struggles to forgive himself, so of course he doesn't believe anyone else can. But I believe he's changed enough during his time at Lives that he'll be able to accept what happened. Perhaps one day soon he'll be able to let it go."

"You have quite a talent for reaching kids' hearts, Grant Adams," she said in a soft voice but meaning every word. "We're blessed to have you in our town."

"I'm a blessing to you, Dahlia?" he teased with a wide-eyed, pretend-innocence look.

"Oh, stop. And yes, you are. And you could be even more of a blessing," she told him, loving this repartee between them.

"Tell me more." He leaned his elbows on the counter and cupped his chin in them.

"I'm planning on going to Lives early tomorrow morning before the store opens. I'll check out the track. If it looks okay, the boys can take out that kart they've repaired and give it a run on Sunday afternoon. Want to come with me?"

Grant smiled. "To see your dream become a reality? I wouldn't miss it."

His words nearly made her heart sing. "Want to bring the girls over for dinner?" she asked without thinking.

"Tonight? But you've been working all day," Grant protested.

Dahlia shrugged. "I put a chicken in the slow cooker at noon so making dinner isn't a big deal." His hesitation made her add, "Please come. I'd appreciate the company." She swallowed past the lump in her throat. "My brother died twelve years ago today."

"I'm so sorry, Dahlia." He reached out and covered her hand with his. His reassuring voice warmed the cold, sad part of her heart that still mourned.

"Of course we'll come," he said, adding, "The girls will love it."

Dahlia found herself hoping that he was going to love it, too.

Her mind drifted back to the night he'd asked her to marry him. It seemed like a long time ago now. How long would their friendship last if another woman came into the picture? How would she feel?

What were they doing?

Dahlia drew her hand away on the pretext of handing him his receipt though she really wanted to hang on and pretend she had the right to.

"I hope Glory and Grace love the sleds," she said, trying to get her mind back on track.

"They will. Christmas is coming so fast." He smiled. "A year ago I couldn't have imagined how my life would change."

"Neither could I."

How could she have imagined the difference Grant and his twins would make to her world?

His gaze held hers. "Your staff is watching us."

Dahlia grinned. "I know." Let them stare. Grant made her feel special and Dahlia didn't want that to end.

"You probably need to get back to work if you're leaving early. And I have some more errands to run while the twins are practicing for the Sunday school Christmas concert. See you at six-thirty?" He murmured the last part in a whisper so her staff couldn't hear.

Her heart thumped at the gentle glow in his eyes.

"Perfect." Dahlia kept her gaze on him until he went out the door. She busied herself counting receipts, urging the clock to hurry toward six-thirty.

Her eagerness to have dinner with Grant was silly. She wasn't what he needed. But she ached to share his life, to know he'd always be there. Until he distanced himself, Dahlia intended to enjoy every moment she had with him.

She locked up the store a few minutes before six, something she'd always before refused to do. At home, she hurried to shower and change, choosing her most flattering outfit. She set the table carefully, with candles and Granny Bev's best dishes, to make the evening special.

Everything Dahlia did now was for Grant. He was in her heart.

When she opened the door and saw him standing there, her pulse skittered. "Welcome!"

His hand rested against hers when he handed over his coat. The contact sent a rush of longing straight to Dahlia's heart. She hid her emotions as the twins enveloped her in hugs. If only this was her family. If only she deserved them.

"Are you sick, Dally? You look funny." Glory peered into her face.

"You're supposed to say she looks nice," Grant said with a rueful shake of his head.

"I'm fine, Glory. Just thankful to have you here." She brushed through the silken curls with her fingers. "Did you have a good day?"

The twins told her about the concert practice at church, and their parts in it. It was a glorious meal, full of intimacy and sharing, as if they were a real family. And through it all, Grant sat watching her, his gaze warm. But when Glory could no longer smother her yawns and Grace nodded off while eating her last bite of the chocolate cake Grant brought, Dahlia knew they'd soon leave.

Loneliness waited to engulf her.

Grant went out to warm up the car and returned shivering.

"The car's thermometer says it's minus thirty-two," he said frowning. "Can that be right?"

"Of course not." Dahlia chuckled. "It was raining when I got up this morning. Even in Churchill the temperature doesn't drop that fast."

"I guess I should get it checked." Grant started to dress the weary twins.

"This will keep you warm, Grace." Dahlia tied her scarf. "Can I have a hug good-night?"

Tiny arms slipped around her neck as a tired voice mumbled good-night. Glory, who usually wiggled nonstop, barely moved between yawns.

"Poor things." Dahlia let them go and rose. "Time for bed. Thanks for coming, Grant."

He stared into her eyes for a long moment. Then he stepped forward to lay his hand against her waist. "Thank you for a wonderful evening, Dahlia."

He kissed her—a gentle, bittersweet kiss that made her want to weep when he finally drew away.

Dahlia could barely catch her breath as she stared into his gentle gray eyes.

"I'm tired, Daddy. Does Dally need another good-night kiss?" Glory asked.

Dally did, but she only smiled as Grant gathered one girl in each arm and went out into the cold.

Then the door closed behind him and she was left alone with one question.

Why had Grant kissed her like that?

Kissing Dahlia like that had rocked Grant's world so badly, he held an all-night vigil to figure out the state of his heart. By morning he was no clearer on how he'd fallen in love; he only knew that it would not go away even if he wished it so, which he didn't.

His feelings for Dahlia were not the same as those he'd had for Eva. He'd lost the desperation that once plagued him. He didn't need Dahlia to rescue him or teach him or save him. Grant needed Dahlia because his life wasn't complete without her. He wanted to share special moments with her. But mostly Grant wanted to fill her world with joy as she filled his.

He loved her.

With a sense of wonder, he prayed for understanding. He knew that God had blessed him because he'd never expected to feel like this about anyone.

Wasn't it about time he told her how her felt?

While the twins slept, Grant savored his first cup of morning coffee and planned how he'd tell Dahlia what lay in his heart. He wasn't a romantic man, but romance was what he wanted for her.

He stood to put his cup in the sink and checked the thermometer. Minus forty degrees? Immediately his thoughts went to Dahlia's track. How had it fared in such cold after so much rain?

Grant set down his coffee. He couldn't let Dahlia go look at it by herself. If something had happened she'd be decimated. He needed to be with her, to support her, to do whatever he could to help.

How quickly Dahlia had become part of his heart, his world, and hopefully his future.

He picked up the phone and dialed. "Lucy, would you be able to come watch the girls this morning?" Only after her groggy voice agreed did Grant realize that it was far too early to phone anyone on a Saturday morning.

But Lucy made it in half an hour, and Grant arrived at Dahlia's house just before eight o'clock. Her truck was running, the windshield clear of frost. As he waited for her to emerge, Grant prayed wordlessly that when he told her how he felt, she'd return his feelings.

In the midst of his pondering, Dahlia stepped

outside and pulled her front door closed. She was drawing on thick gloves when she saw him. Her eyes widened. Grant climbed out of his car and tromped over the icy ground toward her.

"What's wrong?" she asked.

"Nothing. I'm going with you to check out the track. Okay?"

"Sure." She didn't look at him as they climbed in the truck, but Grant put it down to shyness after their kiss. "The ice will come into the harbor now," she murmured. "The polar bears will soon hibernate. Then they won't hurt anyone else."

"Yes." Grant hated the thread of worry in her voice.

Oh, Lord, help, his heart begged.

As they drove to the track, Grant was conscious of tension between them. In silence, they bounced and jounced over the frozen hillocks of tundra until they came to the track. Carefully Dahlia eased her truck onto the asphalt they'd resurfaced. She drove slowly.

"Everything seems okay."

Grant thought so, too, but worry lingered. As faint traces of morning light began to penetrate the gloom, he peered through the windshield, trying to more fully assess the condition of the track.

Suddenly Dahlia jammed on her brakes. She

struggled for a moment to control the sliding vehicle until the wheels found traction and jerked to a stop.

"Oh, no," she gasped.

Grant's breath stopped. Unwilling to accept what he saw, Grant got out of the truck and walked several yards. His heart sank to his toes. A huge section of jagged pavement had heaved upward, probably due to freezing and swelling in the soggy permafrost beneath. The track would have to be completely rebuilt and repaved.

Dahlia's voice was stark with pain. "I couldn't make it happen."

"Now you're responsible for the weather?" Grant couldn't stand to see her so defeated. "You did your best."

"It wasn't enough. It never is." She trudged back to the truck, climbed inside and waited until he joined her before she turned around and drove back.

"So you don't believe God's in control?" he asked when they'd reached the edge of town.

"If He is, where is He now?" Anger tinged her voice.

"Right here. Always has been." Grant couldn't bear to see Dahlia's faith weaken when she'd been such a bulwark to him in his worst moments. "Just because this didn't turn out as you wanted doesn't mean He isn't in it. God has a plan, Dahlia. You helped me see that, remember? Nothing you've done for the boys will be wasted. Somehow He will use this."

She pulled up in front of her house, shoved the gearshift into park and turned on him.

"I don't need platitudes, Grant," she said, her voice tight. "That track was my dearest goal and God abandoned me when I counted on Him most. It's just like with my parents, all over again. They'll arrive to see that once more, poor Dahlia wasn't strong enough."

"But you haven't failed," Grant insisted. "This isn't over yet. You're talking yourself into defeat before the game is finished."

"I am finished. I'm out of money and time."

"God isn't." He grasped her shoulder, turning her to face him. There were tears clinging to her lashes. He caught them on his finger, feeling her pain as his own. "Dahlia, this is the job God laid on your heart, right? Don't be intimidated because things haven't gone the way you wanted."

Her lips pressed together. "I didn't do this only for me— The boys are going to be crushed, Grant."

He pressed his finger to her lips.

"If *God* is for you, who could be against you? It's not you who can make this project succeed, but Him. You have to trust Him. You can do that."

"You have a lot of faith in Him, and me."

"Yes, I do." He cupped his hands around her face and leaned forward, pressing his lips to hers. "Don't give up. Trust Him to come through for you. You're so precious to God." Grant took a deep breath. "And to me, too, my dearest Dahlia."

Dahlia seemed to freeze.

"Wh-what are you saying, Grant?"

He grazed his fingertip over her lovely cheek, quelling his nervousness.

"My feelings have been growing since I first met you on the train, only I didn't know what they were. I've admired your generosity and dedication, the way you challenge and uplift, the way you've taught me how to open myself to what God has given me. You're part of my life and my heart."

Dahlia seemed speechless so Grant continued.

"You are a champion. You're pure and gentle, but you endure like steel." He gazed into her gorgeous eyes, willing her to see how much he cared. "You've become my best friend, the person I want to run to when life overwhelms me. I want to be there for you, Dahlia. I want to share your goals and dreams and your future. You're very special to me, and… I love you."

Dahlia didn't say anything. Grant's nerves stretched piano-wire taut. He needed to hear the words his soul craved—that she loved him.

Finally he asked, "Do you feel anything for me, Dahlia?"

Her slow smile brought joy to his heart. "I've come to treasure you, Grant." Her smiled faded. "But I'm not who you need for the twins."

Grant clasped her hand in his. "Don't talk to me about the twins or anything else. Just tell me. Do you love *me?*" Grant wasn't giving up. Dahlia mattered too much. He felt as if he was holding on to a cliff by his fingernails. One wrong word and she could send him crashing down.

"I do love you, Grant. I love you very much."

Dahlia loved him! His soul sent a praise of thanksgiving. But when he moved to wrap his arms around her, she held up a hand.

"But that doesn't matter."

"It matters more than anything."

"I have a business that takes a lot of time. I—"

"Stop, Dahlia." He frowned. "Tell me the truth."

She bowed her head. Her words came slowly.

"I can't be who you need, Grant. For so long, I felt like I was under Charles's or my parents' thumb, like I needed them to fall back on because I'm not strong. My parents were right."

"You are the strongest woman I know," Grant insisted.

"You think I'm strong because I helped you with the twins." She shook her head. "But inside I'm not like that, Grant."

"Dahlia—"

"I pretend I'm strong because that's the only way I know to get through things. But it's a lie. I don't have the strength to…share my heart with you."

Grant was feeling so much, he hardly knew where to start. And then it became clear.

"Can I say one thing, Dahlia?" At her nod, Grant brushed a curl off her beautiful face. "The reason I said I love you has nothing to do with my daughters. I didn't fall in love with you because you inspired confidence in me, or because you showed me that God is not like my father and that I don't have to try to attain His attention or worry that I'm not a good enough son. I do love you for doing all those things," he said, pressing a kiss to her hand. "But that's not the reason I need you in my life."

She frowned at him, uncertainty coloring her eyes.

"I love you and want you in my life because I can't visualize a future without you, Dahlia.

You are the most important part of my world." He pulled her into his arms and held her tightly, breathing the words into her ear. "I don't need you to be strong. And I understand what it's like to be scared to love. But I need *you,* Dahlia. I love you."

Grant eased her away and then, pressing his lips against hers, tried to show her the depth of his feelings. Gradually Dahlia began to respond, her lips melting against his, sharing the love that surged in his heart. Hope built. Maybe, maybe—

Suddenly it was over.

"I'm sorry, Grant. I can't. I'd fail you, too." She pulled away from him, her face averted, her voice hoarse. "And I couldn't stand that."

She had to get to work so Grant decided to let it go. For now. He climbed out of her truck. "If you need me—" he began.

"I won't. I can't. In fact, I think it's better if we don't see each other," Dahlia whispered. "I'm sorry."

His heart aching, he closed the door and watched her drive away.

At first loss overwhelmed Grant as he pushed through days without Dahlia. But talking to Rick helped him realize that he could no more force her to accept his love than she could force the weather to change. Grant would have to trust God to work on Dahlia.

Meanwhile, Grant was going to prove his love to her.

He gathered together leaders in the community to brainstorm how they could make Dahlia's go-kart track functional. Everyone brought their best ideas, but no matter how hard they tried, they could not figure a way to finish the job.

"There has to be something else we can do," Rick said.

"I agree. We can't just let this die." Laurel studied him. "Are you sure you've thought of everything?"

"Maybe there's a way we could honor her," Mindy suggested.

"Yes. Because her project can't just die," Eddie, the miner, grumbled. "Isn't there someone whose opinion Dahlia values, someone who could help her realize how strong she is."

Then Grant had idea. That night, after the twins were in bed, he made a call.

"Hello, this is Grant. I'm a friend of Dahlia Wheatley's. You're Dahlia's mother, correct?" He held his breath, wondering if the woman would even speak to him. This was his last hope, a desperate move to prove his love to Dahlia.

"She misses you and your husband very much. I know there was a rift between you. I'm hoping this might be the time to repair it."

"Who are you?" the querulous voice demanded.

"I'm the man who loves Dahlia more than anything else in the world. I want her to be happy and I don't think she will be as long as she's estranged from you." Grant took a deep breath. "I'm hoping we can work together to make a very big dream of hers come true."

No response. Defeated, he was ready to hang up when another voice came on the line.

"Tell us what our daughter needs," a man ordered.

Praying for help, Grant explained Dahlia's goal.

Chapter Fifteen

For Dahlia, Christmas had always been a season of joy and excitement. But as December passed, she couldn't find her Christmas spirit. Each day she forced herself to smile and wish her clients merry Christmas while inside her heart shriveled a little more.

Every day, she questioned her decision to refuse Grant's love, but she knew in her heart it had been the right one. She couldn't be a wife and a mother without love, not even for Grant whom she loved deeply. And Grant didn't love her. He couldn't. Not the real, weak her.

Dahlia decorated the sleds he'd ordered, wrapping them with giant shiny bows, green for Glory, red for Grace. When he came to pick them up, she stayed in the stockroom until he left because it hurt too much to see his handsome face.

She'd taken to slipping into church at the last

minute and slipping out again before the services ended to avoid him, too. At the choir cantata featuring the Lives boys, tears welled at the sight of Arlen glowing with happiness because his mother had come for a visit. His deep bass voice underpinned the others', his confidence obvious. She knew he would leave soon to be with his mother. It was best for him, but it was like the final nail finishing her dream to adopt.

"We're caroling tonight." Marni's morning call had come just as she was leaving for work. "You're coming, right?"

"Sorry, I'm too busy." Dahlia didn't have the heart to sing with her friends. "Next year," she promised.

The night of the Sunday school concert, Dahlia crept into church after the lights dimmed. She'd planned to stay away until the twins phoned.

"Please come and see us, Dally," they'd begged. "We have new dresses and we're going to say a poem. Please?"

She couldn't refuse. She smiled, her heart aching when Glory and Grace walked onto the stage. Grant had dressed them in white lacy dresses with green trim and white patent-leather shoes. They looked adorable. Her heart swelled with pride as they recited a sweet, funny poem about love. The poignant words hit deeply, especially the part about trusting that God would make the bad parts better. If only He would.

Dahlia praised them on her way out. But then they begged her to stay and taste the cookies they'd made with their dad. Dahlia couldn't leave, not when Grant added his urging.

"I didn't think you'd come," he said, staring into her eyes.

"I couldn't disappoint the twins. Besides, I wanted to see their new dresses."

"You wanted to see them, but not me."

Another time she might have pretended it wasn't true. But the stark sound of hurt in his words silenced her.

"When will you trust, Dahlia? What do I have to do to prove I love you for yourself? Christmas is a time to believe. Can't you believe in me, just a little?"

"Believing in *you* isn't the issue," she murmured.

"I'm not giving up. Not ever," he said tenderly. "If you can't be strong right now, that's okay. I'll be strong enough for both of us." He kissed her lightly, then drew away. "I love you, Dahlia. Trust God. He won't let you down."

Scarlet-cheeked and aware of interested stares, Dahlia hugged each girl, then hurriedly left, racewalking home through the snow to stop her thudding heart.

Oh, why did he have to kiss her?

She couldn't shake off the ache that kiss engendered. Nor could she sleep later. Overhead, the northern lights danced and twirled in a vortex of green and silver. God had made them. He'd made the universe. He'd made her. Why wouldn't He help her?

Frustrated Dahlia finally flicked on her bedside lamp and grabbed her Bible. An old church bulletin fell out on the floor. Curious, she picked it up. The verse on it blazed at her.

Despite all these things, overwhelming victory is ours through Christ who loved us.

Despite all these things—what did that mean? She turned to Romans 8 and began to read. *For his sake we must be ready to face death.* God wasn't asking her to do that, but Paul had and still he'd been able to say that victory, actually *overwhelming* victory was his.

Dahlia continued reading to the last verse of the chapter. *Nothing can ever separate us from the love of God.*

The strength in those words hit home. She wasn't alone. God had given her work, friends and—dare she believe it?—the love of a man whose integrity was unquestionable. The problem wasn't Grant or the go-kart track or anything else. The problem was her.

God loved her. If she loved Grant, God had

blessed her with the love she'd longed for her entire life. Why not embrace it?

"Because I'm scared I'll fail him, drive him away," she whispered.

Dahlia finally saw the truth. When she didn't get her way, when things didn't go the way she wanted, she blamed God! God didn't need her or the track. But He could use them for His glory, if she let Him.

"I've been a spoiled child." She gazed at the whorls of color that danced in front of her window. "If it doesn't go my way, I don't want to play. I'm running away, just like I did before."

Saying the words aloud brought home the truth. In that moment, Dahlia begged forgiveness.

"The project is Yours, to do with as You please. I relinquish all control. Your will be done."

Grant's face swam into view, his silver-gray eyes brimming with love—for her.

"You know how much I want to trust his love. So I'm asking You to work things out. I will trust You."

Dahlia opened her eyes. Outside, the heavens glowed. A shooting star arced overhead as if to celebrate her surrender. Her fears drained away.

She watched the lights far into the night, glorying in the freedom she now felt. Over and over

Dahlia gave her inadequacies to God, clinging to one verse as she finally allowed herself to bask in the true joy of Christmas.

Overwhelming victory is ours.

Grant was worried. He never should have done it. He was risking everything. If it went badly, he'd lose her forever.

Please don't let that happen.

As he drove to the airport on Christmas Eve morning, all he could do was pray that God would work everything out and that Dahlia would forgive him.

Behind him, the twins chattered gaily. At the airport, they asked questions. He shushed them, promising to explain later. Then the plane pulled in and it was too late to second-guess his actions.

"Hi, I'm Grant," he greeted them inside the tiny airport.

"Good to meet you." Dahlia's father, a tall thin man, held out his hand. His grip was firm. "Where's my daughter?"

"She still—uh, doesn't know you're here," Grant explained.

"I expect she's still angry," her mother said. "We hurt her badly, I'm afraid."

At least they regretted what the past had done to Dahlia, Grant thought, liking the pair but still nervous about their reunion with their daughter. Dahlia's parents gushed over the twins. He drove the couple to the hotel where he told them his plan and their part in it before he took the twins home later to prepare for the Christmas Eve service.

"Daddy, will Dally be happy her mommy and daddy are here?" Glory's forehead furrowed in concern.

"I hope so." Grant prayed fervently that "Dally" would soon be very happy.

Dahlia ached to talk to Grant, but he hadn't answered her messages. In the flurry of last-minute shoppers, Dalia wondered if her hesitation with Grant had cost her everything.

Heart aching, Dahlia reminded herself that God had everything under control. She kept a smile on her face, wishing everyone a merry Christmas. Around three o'clock, the last customer left. She was closing up when Arlen walked in.

"Arlen! I thought you'd gone home. When will that be?" she asked.

"New Year's. My mom's here for Christmas."

"That's nice." Dahlia frowned. Arlen seemed oddly uncomfortable, and wouldn't quite look at her. "Is anything wrong?"

"Kind of." He pulled a package from behind

his back. "I really want to see the track again before I go, just to have a memory to keep. It got be pretty important, you know. My run-in with that polar bear really got me thinking about the future. I'm sorry it's ruined 'cause it would have been cool, but I was wondering—"

"Of course I'll give you a ride out there though I don't know if we'll see much. The days are so short now." She finished closing up and followed him to the front door. The streets of Churchill were nearly deserted. "I guess everyone has finally finished their shopping," she said with a smile. "I've never seen the town look so deserted."

Arlen was silent during the drive but seemed to come alive when she pulled through the fence gates he opened.

"We won't be able to stay long," Dahlia warned. "You guys are singing in the Christmas Eve service tonight and I know you—" The rest of her words dropped away as she turned into the track site and saw the number of cars parked there.

"Come on," Arlen said. "Let's go see what's happening." A funny grin creased his stern face. "Look."

Dahlia followed the direction in which he pointed. The last rays of sunlight highlighted a figure coming toward her. Grant. She'd know that stride anywhere. Her heart swelled with love and then pain. Her fingers tightened around the steering wheel as she fought the urge to put the truck in gear and leave.

Hadn't she promised God she was trusting him?

Arlen climbed out of the truck, and suddenly Grant was there, opening her door, smiling that gorgeous smile. He held out a hand to help her out of the truck. His fingers tightened around hers. And now she recognized the light in his eyes. Love. For her.

"I have a surprise," he whispered.

She gulped then slid her hand in his and stepped down.

"Your parents are here. Everyone is." He turned her to face them. Her parents stood in front of the group, and to Dahlia's astonishment they began to clap. Everyone did. "They're here to honor you."

"Me?" She frowned at him. "Why?"

"Because you're Churchill's citizen of the year, a designation given to the person whose efforts have contributed greatly to the community and its spirit."

"But..." she whispered, trying to understand.

Grant drew her forward, helping her onto the track. The spot where it had heaved had been cleared.

"Grant asked us to come and celebrate your achievement." Her father stepped forward. "We're grateful to him for inviting us to celebrate your honor, Dahlia."

"But the track isn't finished," she sputtered in confusion. "We—I ran out of money."

"In a community like this where the spirit of caring is so strong, money is the least of your worries," her father said. "This track is work to be proud of, Dahlia. It's a goal your mother and I would like to share in, if you'll allow us."

"How?" Dahlia asked, not quite able to grasp all that was happening.

"We'd like to make a donation that will see the completion of your track," her father explained. "If you agree, a paving company will arrive in the spring and lay as much new track as necessary for your go-karts. We're making this donation as a tribute to you, Dahlia, and to Lives Under Construction, because we love you and support you."

The tenderness in his voice stunned her.

"You're a daughter to be proud of." Her mother stepped forward. "We've always regretted that we never gave you enough credit." She shook her head. "We're so sorry, honey. And so proud. You moved here and used that indomitable inner strength of yours to create something lasting." Her mother's eyes filled with tears.

"Your Granny Bev must be celebrating in heaven over you, Dahlia." Tears glittered in her father's eyes, too. "Will you forgive us? Will you allow us to share in this project of your heart?"

"Of course," Dahlia said. "You're welcome here." She threw herself into her parents' arms as peace filled her heart. "I love you guys."

Around her, the crowd cheered. Finally Laurel managed to be heard. She thanked Dahlia for all her hard work, presented her with a plaque on behalf of the town and then invited everyone to Lives for a celebratory snack before the Christmas Eve service at the church.

At Lives, Dahlia was stunned to learn the lengths Grant had gone to in order to locate her parents in Florida without her assistance, and bring them here.

Dahlia couldn't stop smiling. Grant had done this for her because he truly loved her. And she loved him. She ached to tell him so. Her heart sank when Laurel told her he'd already left to get the twins ready for the service. She hadn't even had the chance to properly thank him yet for all that he'd done.

"We should go, too, honey," her mother said. "We don't want to miss Churchill's Christmas Eve service. We've heard it's very special."

"It is," Dahlia agreed. Just then, Arlen appeared with a box.

"I want to give you this." He opened the lid and lifted out a rose bowl with a gorgeous tangerine rose nestled inside. "To thank you. You and Grant helped me change. I came here believing I was alone, but how could I be alone when you kept pestering me?" He grinned.

"Oh, Arlen." Dahlia inhaled the rich scent of the gorgeous flower. "I'm really glad you're going home." She had no regrets. God had a plan for Arlen, too. "Come back and visit us," she said, giving him a hug.

"I'll be here for the opening of the track." He tolerated her hug, then hurried away, red dots of color on each cheek.

"What a lovely boy," her mother said.

Dahlia smiled, remembering how unlovely Arlen had been.

As she drove her parents to her house, her thoughts turned to Grant, and everything he'd done for her.

She couldn't wait to tell him how much she loved him. She only hoped it wasn't too late.

Grant pulled up in front of the church.

"You can't tell anyone," he reminded the twins.

"We know what to do, Daddy," Glory promised.

"We won't tell anyone." Grace's nose wrinkled. "Not even Miss Lucy?"

"Not anyone. Okay?" He tried to be satisfied with their nods.

Praying his scheme would work, he helped the twins from the car and escorted them backstage. Then he found a seat where he could watch Dahlia, who was up front with her parents. His heart hurt from the burgeoning love inside, but, as Glory would say, it was a good hurt.

The kids' choir filed in, backed by the teen group of mostly Lives boys. Rick led everyone in "Silent Night." When the congregation was seated, the lights dimmed and the choir filled the little stone church with glorious music.

Grant imagined that night when God the Father had sent His son to earth. For him. A sweet certainty filled him. He *could* be the father the twins needed because he had his Heavenly Father to lean on. He *could* be what Dahlia needed—with God's help.

When the service ended everyone rose, took a cup holding a lighted candle and paraded through the town to the huge Christmas tree in the square. The group circled the big, lit tree singing "O Holy Night." After wishing each other merry Christmas, the crowd dispersed.

"You know what to do?" he asked the twins as he took their candles.

"We know, Daddy." They waited until he'd

moved out of sight before racing toward Dahlia. "Merry Christmas, Dally." Their voices rang out in the frosty air like joyful bells.

Grant hurried toward the manger scene in front of the church to wait.

Dahlia took her time arriving. When she saw him waiting by the wooden donkey, she paused before continuing toward him.

"Your parents took the twins?" he asked, just to make sure the girls followed orders to go home with Dahlia's parents as soon as they'd delivered their message to Dahlia.

She nodded.

"Good." He took her hands in his, strong hands that gave so much. He placed a kiss in each gloved palm, then pressed her fingers around it. Dahlia's eyes widened, but she said nothing.

"My beloved Dahlia." He couldn't stop staring at her, so lovely in her long green coat and matching beret. "Do you know that you make my world live? You've taught me to see my possibilities in God, to understand that with God's help, I can be the man He wants. But what you doubted is that with God's help, I can also be the man you need."

"Grant—"

He leaned forward and kissed her, lightly, tenderly.

"Let me say this," he begged and waited for her nod. "I love you. You, Dahlia. If you'll trust me, I can change to be what you need."

"No." Dalia shook her head, her hazel eyes glossy with tears. When she tugged her hands from his, Grant thought his heart would crack, until she cupped her fuzzy white gloves against his cold cheeks and pressed a kiss to his lips. "Don't change, Grant. Don't ever change. You're the man of my heart, the one I trust completely."

He was speechless.

"I was wrong, Grant. I was afraid and hurt and so scared to trust that you could love me. But I know now that with you and God, I can accomplish whatever God wills."

She kissed him again, showing her love so sweetly.

"I thought I had to be strong to be used of God. I've come to understand that God works with weakness to make great things. My future plans are now subject to His approval," Dahlia whispered.

"Am I part of your future plans?" he asked softly.

"Without you, I don't have any plans."

"I love you, Dahlia Wheatley." Grant drew her into his arms and kissed her. His dearest wish had come true.

It was only when she finally drew away that

Grant noticed it was snowing, hard. As in blizzard. Dahlia's gorgeous auburn curls were covered in white crystals. She looked like a snow princess.

He felt like her prince.

"Are you going to marry me, Dahlia?"

"Yes." She laughed before sliding her hands around his waist. "Is the deal off if I tell you I want brothers or sisters for the twins?"

For a moment, Grant's heart raced. How could he be a father to more children when he struggled so much with being the right father for the twins?

Then he saw the manger scene and the spotlight shining on it. God would supply all the knowledge Grant would need to raise a family. Hadn't He done that so far?

"My darling Dahlia, you and I are going to have the family that God gives us, whatever its size," he told her as assurance swept through him.

After one last lingering embrace, they hurried arm in arm through the whirling snow to Grant's house, where Dahlia's parents sat reading to the sleepy twins in front of the fire.

As Grant sat beside Dahlia, their hands entwined. They listened to the age-old story of love from heaven. He could hardly wait for tomorrow when Dahlia would open her Christmas gift and find the engagement ring he'd bought for her. Their future would be anchored in the Father's love. Nothing from Grant's or Dahlia's past could ruin that.

Epilogue

On the longest day in June, Dahlia clung to her father's arm as they followed Grace and Glory down the aisle—the aisle being the now-finished Damon Wheatley Go-Kart Track.

The girls had chosen pink dresses and pink shoes. They carried little nosegays of palest pink rosebuds. Dahlia wore a blush-pink ankle-length dress with a silk organza overlay. She carried one bright pink rose.

With the community in attendance, Rick officiated as Dahlia and Grant pledged their love to each other.

"I promise to love you, cherish you, honor you and always believe in you. I promise that together we will teach our children to love God. I love you, Dahlia."

"I promise to trust you no matter what and to love you forever. I promise to be by your side through whatever God sends our way. I love you, Grant."

When Rick pronounced them husband and wife, the audience rose and clapped. A sudden roar of an engine came from the end of the track. Then Arlen, who'd returned for the wedding by special request of the couple, burst over the smooth pavement to run the first lap of the new track in a freshly painted, perfectly humming go-kart.

"Did you know?" Dahlia asked her new husband.

"No clue. Pretty cool way to open the track, huh?"

"Way cool," she agreed as everyone clapped when Arlen returned, grinning from ear to ear.

Dahlia and Grant celebrated their marriage in a reception at Lives, reveling in the support they received, but eager to be alone together. They snuck away after cutting their cake. Dahlia's parents drove them to the train station.

"You have our phone numbers," Dahlia said to her parents. "If anything happens with the twins, you promise to call?"

Glory tugged on her new grandmother's skirt. "Do they know about the boat ride we're going to take?" she whispered.

"Boat ride?" Grant asked carefully. "What boat ride?"

"To see the whales," Grace explained. "It's a blow-up boat. A Zoe-something. I hope the whales don't poke a hole in it."

"I hope you don't fall out," Glory said.

Grant opened his mouth just as the train whistled. Dahlia leaned over, kissed his cheek and reminded him, "We're leaving things up to God, remember? He surely knows how to care for two little girls."

"I have a hunch it's your parents who will need looking after," Grant told her.

They got on the train in a flurry of confetti and took seats by the window, where they could wave goodbye until the train slowly pulled out of the station.

"I love you," Dahlia whispered.

"I love you," Grant replied.

The bride and groom were oblivious to the other passengers as they stared into each other's eyes while the train rumbled over the tracks, taking them away from the tiny town where they would create their first home together.

"They're all looking at us, you know," Dahlia whispered after a quick glance around the train car.

"They're looking at you, the most beautiful woman in the world," Grant corrected.

"Thank you, darling." Dahlia returned his kiss then laid her head on his shoulder to watch the taiga give way to trees as the midnight sun shone on. Suddenly she sat up. "I never did find out where you're taking me for our honeymoon."

"Banff." He waited for the smile to light the flecks of gold in her eyes.

"Really?" A smile spread across her lips.

"I know how much you love nature, and I have it on good authority that the stargazing is unbelievable." Grant snugged his arm around her.

"'The heavens declare the glory of God.' They're a marvelous display of His handiwork," Dahlia murmured. "It's the perfect place to thank God for all He's done for us." She leaned over to kiss Grant's cheek.

Grant turned his head just in time to catch her kiss. When it ended, they heard the woman behind them sigh and say, "Love. Nothing can beat that gift from God."

Grant smiled at Dahlia, who nodded in perfect agreement.

* * * * *

Get 4 FREE REWARDS!

We'll send you 2 FREE Books plus 2 FREE Mystery Gifts.

FREE Value Over **$20**

Both the **Love Inspired**® and **Love Inspired**® Suspense series feature compelling novels filled with inspirational romance, faith, forgiveness, and hope.

YES! Please send me 2 FREE novels from the Love Inspired or Love Inspired Suspense series and my 2 FREE gifts (gifts are worth about $10 retail). After receiving them, if I don't wish to receive any more books, I can return the shipping statement marked "cancel." If I don't cancel, I will receive 6 brand-new Love Inspired Larger-Print books or Love Inspired Suspense Larger-Print books every month and be billed just $6.24 each in the U.S. or $6.49 each in Canada. That is a savings of at least 17% off the cover price. It's quite a bargain! Shipping and handling is just 50¢ per book in the U.S. and $1.25 per book in Canada.* I understand that accepting the 2 free books and gifts places me under no obligation to buy anything. I can always return a shipment and cancel at any time by calling the number below. The free books and gifts are mine to keep no matter what I decide.

Choose one: ☐ **Love Inspired**
Larger-Print
(122/322 IDN GRDF)

☐ **Love Inspired Suspense**
Larger-Print
(107/307 IDN GRDF)

Name (please print)

Address   Apt. #

City   State/Province   Zip/Postal Code

Email: Please check this box ☐ if you would like to receive newsletters and promotional emails from Harlequin Enterprises ULC and its affiliates. You can unsubscribe anytime.

Mail to the Harlequin Reader Service:
IN U.S.A.: P.O. Box 1341, Buffalo, NY 14240-8531
IN CANADA: P.O. Box 603, Fort Erie, Ontario L2A 5X3

Want to try 2 free books from another series! Call 1-800-873-8635 or visit www.ReaderService.com.

*Terms and prices subject to change without notice. Prices do not include sales taxes, which will be charged (if applicable) based on your state or country of residence. Canadian residents will be charged applicable taxes. Offer not valid in Quebec. This offer is limited to one order per household. Books received may not be as shown. Not valid for current subscribers to the Love Inspired or Love Inspired Suspense series. All orders subject to approval. Credit or debit balances in a customer's account(s) may be offset by any other outstanding balance owed by or to the customer. Please allow 4 to 6 weeks for delivery. Offer available while quantities last.

Your Privacy—Your information is being collected by Harlequin Enterprises ULC, operating as Harlequin Reader Service. For a complete summary of the information we collect, how we use this information and to whom it is disclosed, please visit our privacy notice located at corporate.harlequin.com/privacy-notice. From time to time we may also exchange your personal information with reputable third parties. If you wish to opt out of this sharing of your personal information, please visit readerservice.com/consumerschoice or call 1-800-873-8635. **Notice to California Residents**—Under California law, you have specific rights to control and access your data. For more information on these rights and how to exercise them, visit corporate.harlequin.com/california-privacy.

LIRLIS22R2

HARLEQUIN
PLUS

Announcing a **BRAND-NEW** multimedia subscription service for romance fans like you!

Read, Watch and Play.

Experience the easiest way to get the romance content you crave.

Start your **FREE 7 DAY TRIAL** at
<u>www.harlequinplus.com/freetrial</u>.